MISTY'S PLACE

Dennis A Nehamen

Golden Poppy Publications
Los Angeles

Misty's Place
By Dennis A Nehamen

Copyright © 2016 Dennis A Nehamen
All Rights Reserved

Published by Golden Poppy Publications™
Los Angeles, CA
www.dennisnehamen.com

ISBN: 978-1-945329-00-5

Library of Congress Control Number: 2016906561

Lyrical passages by Craig M Nehamen

Cover by Cline Cover Design

Nehamen, Dennis A Author

Misty's Place

Dennis A Nehamen

1. Fiction
2. Women
3. Contemporary

Printed in the United States of America

First Edition

I'm comfortable saying that nobody will ever read as many manuscript pages of my work as my wife, Bernice. Each novel she proofed, from the earliest versions forward—and I'll admit reworking my stories until they beg to be completed. She's known for her tolerance, and I'm sure I've tested it. Thank you!!

PROLOGUE

The judicial gavel for an entire culture had long before closed debate on the subject of whether or not a child could be properly raised in a brothel. Even Misty would have protested the absurdity of experimenting with bringing an infant into her fine establishment. But there are occasions when destiny's dangling carrots order the most rational thinkers to betray sound judgment.

Further, it's owing to these exceptions to rules that the history of mankind has been blessed with miracles. Misty's Place was about to birth a prodigy.

CHAPTER 1: NOT ALL FUN AND GAMES

Misty's Ranch is a one-of-a-kind establishment. A man of sufficient wealth and power can at any time he chooses, have the best of live entertainment, the finest food and beverage, horseback rides at dusk with luscious ladies, a round of golf with a stunningly beautiful female chauffeuring his cart, poker games with sensual women dealing, and…well, that too.

Misty is a businesswoman. Since establishing this high-class brothel on a five thousand acre ranch in Nevada in 1985, she was generating millions in income. It was more like a country club with the members needing to be sponsored before being able to partake in the festivities.

It was generally a happy and harmonious place. It certainly looked to be on the surface. The girls got along well with each other. There was always a cheery atmosphere. But then again, as is the case with any organization, there might be dark issues betraying the otherwise peaceful ambiance.

In fact, the unfortunate circumstance leading to the drama that was about to unfold began in the main hall of the ranch after what had seemed to be a rapturous evening. It was three in the morning and business had closed. The girls had retired to their rooms…all but one of them. Sadly, Misty kept no priest on staff; she would deliver divine retribution through her own code of justice.

The dark cherry wood bar filtered innumerable shades of red, blue, yellow, purple and green into the room from the liquor bottles reflecting against the glass behind them. As was typically the case, the scent of spirits, smokes and the essence of the various fragrances worn by the ladies that evening lingered like delinquents.

The room was deadly still. Misty was standing at one end with a young girl, Gyps, quaking, across from her boss. It looked like a standoff with neither moving. Misty was glaring while Gyps seemed to be awash in contrition. For several more seconds, the space remained silent. It was the type of cold quietude that begs to hush sin.

"I'm sorry; please, Misty, forgive me," Gyps pled in a near inaudible whisper.

Misty now moved forward, toward Gyp's corner, narrowing the physical distance between them. Misty's jaw was firm, battling to contain hot rage. Halfway across the room she paused, throwing her hands open in an inquisitive gesture.

"Forgiveness?" she screeched. "Again? How many times do I pardon you for your offenses and excuse your irresponsibility? How many times do I give special treatment to an ungrateful child who deserves nothing more than being cast away like the useless slut you are?"

"Misty, all I want to do is keep the baby. I'll go away and take care of it and you'll never hear from me again," Gyps beseeched.

"You've never been able to take care of yourself. You're going to look after an infant?" Misty sneered. She turned away from the girl, in an attempt to calm herself. "Why didn't you tell me earlier? All this time you hid it from me." The harshness of her tone mercilessly pounded the frightened girl. "I could have handled this; you know that."

"I didn't want you to be upset."

"I'm so grateful to you. Can't you see how successful you've been? I'm not the least bit upset," Misty caustically assaulted Gyps with irony.

Gyps knelt down, nearly collapsing from the wickedness of Misty's reproach. Finally, she fell into a sitting position on the ground, cradling the life within her womb. Misty rushed to her, yanking Gyps back onto her feet to face her.

"If it were anyone else, I'd have tossed you out on the street."

"Maybe I'm not as good as you; maybe I'm not as perfect," Gyps weakly defended herself.

"Oh, please, you're perfect," Misty mocked the girl. "You're well into a pregnancy and you know damn well who the father is. Hell. You got yourself knocked up by my business partner, the most influential man in the state..." Misty threw her hands upward in a comical gesture of appreciation. "How much more perfect could you get?"

Gyps fell back to the ground, staring up at the unsympathetic figure hovering over her like a foul prophecy. She was left with no argument, her tears serving only as hope for leniency.

"I'm having you taken away where they'll see to the delivery and have the child placed in a proper home."

"But Misty, it's my—"

"Get out!"

Misty heartlessly casted Gyps out of the room and seemingly out of her life. The lady had a business to run. Compassion? The girls working for her knew the rules; as long as they committed no serious violations they could expect mercy to be dispensed as freely as promises at a political debate. Misty invested heavily in her employees; Gyps in particular. That she couldn't treat the young thing the same as the others nagged at her; yet she knew under the circumstances that true equality was impossible. That's why her level of infuriation had peaked.

*****

Later, it would take only a short announcement to the other girls to explain the abrupt departure of Gyps. Collectively, they understood that Misty was doing what Misty had to do. Still, they anticipated that Gyps would be headed back to the ranch after delivering a baby. The girls asked Misty no questions.

Shortly before the baby was to be born, one of the girls, Crystal, had a brainstorm. She woke up one morning with elements of a dream that wouldn't stop tickling her psyche. It was well over an hour that she lay in bed wrestling with the disconnected images before finally they coalesced into an intelligible whole. She had imagined herself a mother, an unfathomable fantasy she'd have never granted herself in her conscious mind.

As she deliberated what had intruded into her rest, and then lingered in her waking thoughts, she realized that she really wasn't any different from every other woman, even all her "sisters" at Misty's. There was a biological drive to perpetuate the species through procreation, as well as an equally compelling need psychologically to nurture an infant to maturity.

Crystal at the time was only twenty-six. She wondered

if there might still be hope for her, especially knowing that women were giving birth up to age forty without a problem. It was common knowledge that her career at Misty's would be over before that; none of the girls even reached thirty-five before they retired.

Deliberating on the topic was unnerving to her. The more she contemplated her future, the greater were her feelings of sadness. She yearned for motherhood; sooner rather than later. Knowing that was improbable, she tried to douse the pestering fantasy. When she was unsuccessful it frightened her. Then, out of a sense of desperation, the thought of conception triggered a different sort of birthing, an idea she thought might bandage at least for the foreseeable future the sorrow she experienced knowing motherhood had to be well into her future, if at all.

Impossible, she mused to herself. Then she concluded definitively. *Never. She'd never consider it.*

Still, she had conceived a proposition, one that cried out to be expressed. Later that morning at breakfast, she gingerly brought up her dream, and then the stream of thought it had sparked for her.

"Are you thinking what I think you're thinking?" Ricki—one of the other girls—posed tentatively to Crystal.

"Well, what if we all threatened to quit?" Crystal proposed, gagging over the absurd approach.

"I could see it now. Misty would have us packed and hauled off before we finished the proposal," Ricki concluded. "You don't bully Misty, and you don't bluff her either."

"I know," Crystal agreed, "but what if we try begging?"

"We can't do this unless we're all committed," Ricki determined.

"Well?" Honey questioned. "All in agreement raise your left hand."

There were no dissenters.

"You'll have the honor of approaching her," Honey mentioned to Crystal. "That way if she has the urge to punch out the plan, you'll be the one taking her fist first," she chuckled.

About an hour later Crystal, followed by the rest of the girls, meekly knocked on the door to Misty's office.

"Good morning, Misty. We were wondering if we might have a few minutes to talk with you."

"Of course, dear." The door stood fully opened and Misty could see the necks of the rest of the girls craning forward to be able to hear. "All of you? It must be important. I'll meet you in the main room in a couple of minutes."

When Misty entered, the girls were seated around the room. Crystal spoke softly; she tippy-toed her words like gentle steps intended not to arouse a sleeping monster.

"It's about Gyps. We thought maybe—"

"Girls, I really don't want to know what you're thinking," Misty said kindly.

"We thought maybe you might take it easy on her," Toni gently jabbed against the admonition.

"Would I take it easy on any of you?"

The girls knew she wouldn't, and they wisely refrained from pushing the point. In fact, none of them had ever been able to account for the permissiveness that Misty had afforded Gyps in the past, offering amnesty for acts that never would have been allowed for any of the other crew members. The only explanation that had ever rung true was that Gyps was childishly naïve and Misty had a soft spot for her. They were grossly mistaken.

"Misty, it's really not so much about Gyps as the little baby," Crystal spoke.

"The infant will be placed in a loving home," Misty assured them.

"That's exactly what we all want," Crystal said excitedly. "We figured out how to handle it."

"Okay, darling, I'm listening," Misty consented with a grin, her thick lips spreading in laughter.

"We keep the baby and raise it here." Crystal gushed her words. "You see, Misty, we've talked about it. We could make schedules—"

"And divide up responsibilities," Honey added to the pitch.

"Are you all nuts?" Misty gasped. "This is not exactly a nursery. The last thing our customers want waddling around here is a toddler. I can see it now."

This was not the first time Misty had been summoned

by her girls, only to be approached with a half-baked idea that she had to reject. But the nonsensicalness of this one inspired Misty to borrow on her acting skills to teach the girls a lesson that would hopefully avoid future muddleheaded excursions on their part.

Misty was envisioning a diapered infant screaming for a bottle in the middle of a whorehouse. It was a loony image that she embraced, one that thrust her into an impromptu skit. She grabbed Crystal, dragging her along as they approached an imaginary door that Misty swung open. Her hands were indignantly resting on her hips as she stared into the illusory space beyond the door.

"Excuse me, Mr. Lawson," she admonished her make-believe client. "Yes, I know you're primed for action, but it is Tuesday." She turned to address Crystal. "It's Crystal's day to feed the baby."

She continued to upbraid the man. "Mr. Lawson, if you don't mind my saying, you're acting just a bit self-ish. There's a little infant shrieking with hunger and you want to deprive it so you can…Christ, no wonder you disappoint your wife and children."

Misty pretended to slam the door. She then scampered throughout the room, chasing after the fanciful child.

"It'll really get to be fun when the little boy—"

"Boy?!" the girls pondered in unison.

"Well, it could be. And what a celebration for all of us when the grand master runs into Abby's room and sees her naked, in pious worship to Mr. Mitchell, who is standing firm as a baseball bat."

"Oh, mommy, can Abby do that with me too?" Misty imitated the child.

"No silly, you don't have enough money," she answered in her madam role. "But when you grow up and become a rich, powerful man, you'll be able to afford one of the nice girls, like Abby...and Ricki and Crystal and Toni and Vera and Honey too. My god, you can have them all bowing to you."

By now Misty had reclaimed her normal sense of self.

"And what if we have a young belle sprouting up amongst us? Won't it be grand? She'll want to have some of her friends over to play, right?"

Misty positioned herself on the couch. She picked up a book and started reading. Next she acted out picking up the receiver of a ringing phone.

"Hello, Ms. Patterson. You don't say. (Silence.) Julie said she saw what is happening here? (Girls all giggling.) She must be mistaken...or," feigning shock, "she has a vivid imagination. It's true my little Emma has eight sisters but..."her voice rose as she expressed outrage toward the caller, "they're as pure white as an elephant's tusk. And furthermore, I might advise you to be careful with accusations. I never wanted to say it, but your Julie seems rather promiscuous to me." Misty motioned as if she'd slammed down the phone. "Hah, the nerve of that woman."

Misty walked back to the girls and sat again.

"By the time dear Emma is eighteen she can put on a mini skirt and get to work." Misty mused before proceeding. "Gee, I wonder what she'll be doing by the time she's twenty?"

"I'll bet you'd make a great mom, Misty," Crystal cautiously flattered. "Look how you take care of all of us."

"Thank you, but—"

"Misty, please," the girls sung out together, still undaunted by Misty's opposition.

"This little thing will have more love than any baby on earth," Crystal voiced independently.

"It'll be a bright light for Misty's and for all of us," Ricki chimed in.

"I'll think about it," Misty shockingly responded.

The girls couldn't believe what they had heard.

"Really? Wow!" together they shouted gleefully.

They could hardly contain the thrill, dashing out of the room laughing and chattering.

Misty sat by herself, deep in contemplation. It was a wacko idea. The lady had always prided herself on sound, logical decision making. *Live dangerous.* That would never be a maxim for Misty. It was, therefore, a simple matter that deserved no more consideration than applying for pastoral training. But there were special issues at stake that were weighing on her conscience, and they advocated forcefully for their position, and convincingly. She made a last ditch appeal to her hard-core business persona, but she couldn't rally the needed support to nix on-the-spot the girls' proposal.

She smiled. Her thoughts drifted back to her own skits performed moments earlier for the girls; she wondered how close they might be to reality.

Wow! There was a baby coming to Misty's. She, Ricki, Honey, Crystal and the rest of the team were all going to be playing new roles as moms, sisters, aunts, cousins and nannies.

CHAPTER 2: IT'S A...GIRL

Gyps gave birth to a seven pound, six ounce female on July 30, 1993. The little dear was in perfect health. The mother handled the delivery without need for medical intervention other than standard obstetrical assistance.

After the birth, Gyps slipped out of the maternity ward and disappeared. Misty was in the waiting room. When the nurse told her that the mother had left without leaving a message as to where she was headed, Misty was not surprised. She had already insisted that she have legal guardianship over the infant from birth. She advised the hospital representative that she would be taking the baby home as soon as possible.

Two days later, early in the morning, she arrived at the ranch. She drove home and parked in front of the lodge, the tiny baby girl crying in the car carrier she'd purchased the day before. It was the only time in her life she could recall being afraid; sole responsibility for another life was something she'd never anticipated.

Misty was raised in a comfortable environment. Her father was an inventor who had filed patents in the electronics field that quickly became invaluable. He made millions in a matter of a couple years. Misty was sent off to be educated in a private finishing school, and then earned an Ivy League college degree.

It was fifteen years later when her parents, Frank and Sylvia, would have two more children, Misty's only siblings. The firstborn was a girl, followed the next year by a boy. Sadly, the fate of the younger two was not as favorable as for their elder sibling. Shortly after the two were born, her father experienced a dramatic change in personality. From a docile, kindly and introverted man he became hostile and argumentative at first, and later violent.

When Misty would visit the home after her emancipation, she'd be shocked to discover that her father, after a frenzied fit, had beaten her mother, brother and sister. She'd intervene whenever she was present, mitigating the damage to the three other family members, but she had no way of preventing split lips, blackened eyes and bloody noses when she was absent—the younger siblings both seemed to have fragile psyches and over time they weakened and withered.

The brother fared worse. Hopeless under the gravity

of desperation, seeking his father's love, he committed suicide at fourteen years of age. Her sister was fifteen when she lost her brother. One year later, the mother, seeking to follow her son to heaven, also took her own life. The father shortly after that was diagnosed with a malignant brain tumor, answering the mystery of his dramatic character change—he died during surgery not more than six months after his wife took her life. Misty had lost most of her family within a span of a year and a half.

In all fairness, the siblings were more the age of children to her. Still, Misty struggled with feeling that she had committed an unpardonable sin by not removing her brother and sister from the home. She knew it wasn't practical at the time for her to take them, but guilt still weighed on her, at times punishing her that she should have done more.

Her sister having taken to the streets and disappearing did nothing to ease her conscience. She searched in every way possible, but couldn't find the girl. There was a large inheritance that Misty looked after in the absence of her sibling. In fact, both sisters jointly owned the huge parcel of land in Nevada that would ultimately become *Misty's Place*, although the younger sister would have no idea of her wealth.

During this painful episode of her life, Misty had been working at the Remington Hotel in Las Vegas as their marketing director. She became involved in an intimate relationship with the owner. At one point, she approached him about the land, explaining that she was considering selling it. He, in turn, shared with her a business plan that he had put together a year earlier.

Since he owned several of the top local hotels, and had influence with the owners of most of the other high-end establishments, he was sure that the enterprise would thrive. As it turned out, Misty put up the land and he chipped in the money. As a result, a partnership was born. Misty had no knowledge of the prostitution business but assumed it was no different from any other for-profit concern. Her theory proved to be correct.

She recognized early in life that she had little compassion for the common and pathetic excuses that people were willing to grant themselves for their inadequacies. After the tragic losses in her family, her attitude stiffened further. She was still aware, however, that the success of any enterprise rested on the quality of personnel hired to perform the needed functions. She never let her personal suffering interfere with her treatment of her employees. She held them to the highest standard of performance but they were rewarded for their contributions.

Each of the girls had a retirement and savings plan set up in their name. Misty educated them about money management. She assured them that when they retired from their employment they would have amassed enough to live comfortably for the rest of their lives.

It had all been smooth and predictable, except for one gnawing issue.

Misty dwelled on that point as she sat in her car. She was unable to mobilize herself to enter her home with the baby. She couldn't help wondering if she had done wrong, if she had embraced a mistaken philosophy and failed to account for the fact that some people were damaged to the point that they deserved preferential treatment, forever if necessary.

No!! She refused to budge. Gyps had made her own bed and defined her own destiny. She couldn't be granted one additional excuse. It was especially the case due to Misty's generosity where she had given her every opportunity to redirect her life. Misty had stepped out for the girl like she'd never done for another person, and in return what did she have to show for it?

She was exhausted from her dual responsibilities at the ranch and hospital during the past couple of days. But as the last question paraded through her mind, she picked up the infant. The tiny girl represented the answer as to what she had received for her generosity. She bundled the little thing under her arm. It was time to be mommy.

She entered the main room and sat for a few minutes, holding the baby to her chest, listening to the quiet breathing of the fragile creature. Her emotions were stirred. She wouldn't have admitted it but she wanted the warm creature close to her. She wanted to feel the softness of the facial skin against her cheek and smell the scent of rose petals she swore were coming from the little girl's delicate, milky scalp.

For a moment she pulled the baby away, holding her outstretched so she could gaze at her. Her face was perfect, almond colored with cute puffy cheeks. She pulled her knees half way to her chest, creating a ledge to rest the infant so that she could continue to inspect her. She marveled at the silkiness and smoothness of the forehead; she rubbed her fingers gently across it and then let them explore the crown, pressing ever so tenderly on the open spaces of the undeveloped skull.

Misty had an impulse to do what she couldn't remember doing since the first time she witnessed her father smash his fist into her mother's chest and then smack her across the face. She had sobbed. After that tragic experience, she recalled telling herself there was no reason for weeping; there was nobody there who could wipe her tears, let alone comfort her. It was Misty who would minister to her mother's wounds.

Now, with the baby's blank eyes reading her from only a foot away, Misty wanted to cry. She wouldn't have permitted it even if she hadn't been interrupted.

The girls had been eagerly anticipating her return. Then after they knew their boss had arrived, they waited as long as they could tolerate before knocking at the door. Crystal was leading the group. Misty instructed them to enter.

They marched in jubilantly to see the newborn. Misty listlessly passed the little girl to Crystal. So thrilled were the girls that not one noticed the sorrow on Misty's face. They had been preparing for days. The thought of the little one coming to be raised at Misty's had inspired them to create. Together they had even written lyrics and outlined a plan to deliver them to welcome the baby home.

"Imagine what this little thing is gonna turn into," the girls spoke together jubilantly.

Then Crystal held the child outstretched while she added her lines. "One of these days, she's gonna tap my arm to play, and it'll set my heart ablaze, one of these days...not far away," she affirmed to her colleagues before continuing. "One of these weeks she'll speak out, with a tone you couldn't sing, one of these weeks between those cheeks, she's gonna let it ring."

Honey ran over and took the baby, cradling her in her arms as she smiled adoringly at the infant. "One month I got a hunch she'll pack a pretty punch, one of these months she's gonna bite back with a light snap. One year awfully near she'll be off to a career...she'll be at the heart of all you hear," she rejoiced before changing her tone for her final line. "One of these days she'll make me cry without the pain."

"It's my turn," Vera impatiently called out, the baby being passed to her by Honey. "One of these days while I lay, she'll sit next to me and sway, one of these weeks like a treat she'll be prancing at my feet. One of these months when I'm sunk she'll giggle at my funk, one of these years she'll be commonly revered."

All the girls joined together for the final line. "One of these days she'll make us cry without the pain!"

Crystal took the baby again in her arms, staring at Misty. "I see this sweet child's face, the bright smile and the humble shine. She's going to be special."

Misty loved entertainment and had made it a core ingredient for her business. Yet on this occasion, she seemed oblivious to the girls' composition. She was in a funk of her own, not hearing that it is possible to cry without pain, that this child could bring joyful tears.

She was using the time to harden her heart for the assignment she'd been dreading since she was last at the hospital. By the time the recital stopped, she knew there could be no delay.

"Star! We thought we'd talk to Gyps and see what she thinks about naming the baby Star. Wouldn't that be great, Misty?" the girls called out excitedly.

Misty stared at the cheery group pitching a name. Atypically, she found that she couldn't speak. The words that she had prepared coalesced at the back of her throat like phlegm. She coughed but her speech fought back.

"Isn't this great, Misty?" the girls entreated.

She swallowed, trying an alternative strategy to make way for words; still it failed to produce a sound.

"You don't like it, Misty?" Ricki asked.

"Girls," Misty finally responded somberly, "Gyps died giving birth."

There were deep bonds that had developed between the girls. They worked together, played together, entertained together, ate together, took lessons together and slept together under the same roof. Often they'd take trips together during time off. It was not like most brothels where the working ladies had only superficial relationships between themselves. An employee of Misty's became one of the family; they were for the time they worked for Misty, sisters.

Gyps had been the youngest of the group; she had also been with Misty the shortest amount of time. Still, she was adored, much like the little sibling. The news of her passing shocked the girls. But Misty wasn't finished with them.

"I don't want her name ever mentioned here again. Are we understood?" Misty firmly ordered.

The girls had been clutching one another while pitifully sobbing. Hearing Misty's words perplexed them, but none dared question her. They knew who made the rules, and more so how to tell which ones could be tested without punishment. Misty's tone of voice left no doubt the name Gyps would from then on be whispered out of earshot of their madam.

Despondently, they started to leave, Misty still holding the baby as they filed out.

"Star. That's a good name my little doll. I'll keep you

with me. You'll never have to leave here, never have to go where it's unsafe," Misty vowed to her new daughter. She blinked, the repressed tears begging for expression that would go unsatisfied.

Only a few minutes later, Crystal came back hesitantly into the room.

"We'll watch her, Misty, until you feel better if it's okay," she offered, pulling the stick of candy she was sucking out of her mouth.

Misty handed Star over. She sat still for some time, saddened that she had lied to the girls about Gyps, yet at the same time resolved that there had been no other way to handle the situation. It was best to admonish the ladies firmly right from the start and to get the matter over with.

Misty was infuriated about the whole affair. She was also humiliated that Gyps had defied her. That was the end; for all practical purposes, Gyps *was* dead. That's why she told the lie and had to tell it. She confirmed for herself that it was the only sensible thing to do. It was the only way for life to go on and for the baby to stand a chance of bettering the miserable track record of the child's mother.

As she sat thinking, she was distracted by what she believed was the sound of a door handle twisting behind her. Then she heard the gentle creaking of the planks of knotty black alder flooring, confirming to her that somebody had entered without first being given permission: that single fact assuring her that it couldn't have been any of her staff.

Moving slowly, out of her range of vision, was a man in his early fifties. He stood a couple inches over six feet, with a healthy head of thick silver hair that was stylishly cut. He was indistinguishable from one of thousands of middle age handsome men, except...Hugh Crawford was richer and more powerful. It was not only Las Vegas where he held vast parcels of land being leased by luxury hotels, several of which he owned. He was titleholder of many of the prime properties throughout the state and was the majority stockholder in two of the largest forest product companies in the world.

The other venture that he held interest in—half partnership in *Misty's Place*—was a true "silent investment:" the reality was that while there may have been rumors about a romance between them, only Misty and Hugh were aware of their business and personal association.

He approached her and placed his hand on her long, thin shoulder.

"Talk to me, my love. Give me the news," Hugh greeted her gently.

"One of the girls got pregnant," Misty reported indifferently as she twisted her neck to look at her visitor. Her golden-blond hair was pulled off her forehead and held by a forest green stretch band, accentuating features that could earn her a spot on the cover of a glamour magazine.

"With all that protection?" Hugh smirked while musing on the situation. "Little guy must have had heart. Well, you'll handle it."

"Too late. She withheld it from me too long. I had to let her give birth."

Hugh took a stick of gum and unwrapped it, offering one to Misty. She ignored it. Hugh took a seat on the sofa next to Misty.

"She died after the baby was born."

"Oh, god, no. Is the baby okay?"

"Hugh, it's a little girl; healthy, absolutely perfect. She's an angel."

"Misty?" Hugh addressed her inquisitively. "There's more to this story. I never thought I'd hear you express tenderness about a baby."

"That's right, there is a lot more to the story—the child is yours."

"What?!"

"I told you any of the girls but that one were fine for you, but you didn't listen to me, did you?" she spit out at her partner. "She was off all of July and refused to tell me where she went. Then after she was in the hospital I finally pried it out of the little shit, that you had put her up in one of your goddamn resorts so you could fuck her outside of my authority."

"Look, Misty, I didn't understand why you made such a big deal out of her in the first place. Besides, she was the best—"

"I know how terrific she was. But I guess you don't recall our agreement: I run Misty's and everything associated with it," she fumed. "But that wasn't good enough for you, was it? It was none of your business why I made the decisions I did, about that girl or any of the others. I had my reasons for every choice I made. Well, now look where we are."

Hugh stood, motoring around the room.

"My child; a daughter! I'd break into song and dance if it weren't for—"

"Right. One tiny thing, Hugh, you have a family."

"That I do. So? We need to do something here; it's my baby."

"Oh, stop. I've already decided what to do."

"I'm waiting, darling."

"I'm keeping her with me. I'll raise her."

"In a brothel?" Hugh laughed. "Are you out of your senses?"

"Let me explain."

"Wait. What do you want with a baby? You told me you'd make the worst mother this planet has ever seen."

"People change. I've considered this from every angle. I'm going to grow old. One day I'm going to wake up and say to myself, 'My god, you thought you did it exactly how you wanted but you know, you never had the joy of being a mom.' It hit me as I faced this situation. Then after I was holding the infant that was it. I guess an instinct awakened."

"I've never seen you like this," Hugh responded dubiously. "There has to be another chapter to this tale."

"Not a thing," Misty stated emphatically. Then she dwelled on a thought. "I've been mom to every one of my girls. I'll bet if you ask them every last one will tell you I've been better than the woman that birthed them. Maybe I won't be as bad as I thought."

Hugh nodded approvingly, but still pondered the situation circumspectly.

"So how do you plan to pull this off?"

"I'm not—you are."

"No, Misty. This is not the time in my life for scandal, and I'm not up for raising another child."

"I didn't know you raised the one you have," Misty heartlessly stabbed at her partner.

"Well, my wife did a fine job and he and I got on fine too. Some day if you meet my boy, you'll see for yourself. Besides, sons need their dads more when they're grown."

"Okay, look, here's how it's going to work. I have full custody; the kid signed it to me before she died. Now, the father was marked unknown but I want her to have a father of record. It's simple. You're going to adopt the baby under a different name and I'll raise her. Hugh, you can use some of that vast power and influence of yours to work out the kinks."

"For you, my lovely, consider it done."

"There's one other matter. I keep the girl with me.

She'll be here, and as long as that's the case you'll never interfere. You can come visit like you normally might but not let the girl know who you are. I won't compromise here, understood?"

"So do I get to see my girl?"

Misty walked out of the room, returning a few minutes later holding the little one. She handed her to Hugh.

"Your daughter's name is Star."

"Sounds like my girl, a star," he beamed. "Anything she needs, Misty, she gets. I'll pay for whatever it is."

"Aren't you already paying enough, not being able to disclose the fact that you're her father?"

"No problem. I'll be watching the little star grow up. Hell, I'll be like an uncle."

Hugh walked out of the room with a smug look on his face. Misty measured his sense of contentment, wondering how long it would be before she'd have to battle Hugh for control of her child. She knew that he was a man who never surrendered unconditionally and who capitulated only while scheming his next move.

She took a liberty she otherwise never would have allowed herself, pushing the matter out of her conscious awareness prematurely. She was a mom; instincts were already fuddling dangerously with reason.

CHAPTER 3: FINDING HELL

A merciful and loving God might punish Satan for even suggesting the existence of a tormenting, suffering and hateful place called Hell. Yet He might have received a strong affirmation of its reality by Gyps.

After she left the hospital, she fell into a horrid slump. She saw herself as having lost everything. She had once more failed the lady who had repeatedly demonstrated faith in her by coming to her rescue, she had left herself without work or a means of supporting herself in the manner she had been used to living, she had disappointed her friends who had been like sisters but who now she could never contact, and she had walked away from an infant, her only child.

She wandered aimlessly for an amount of time she couldn't estimate. She had no idea what direction she was headed or where she might want to get to. As it happened, a trucker headed to New York picked her up and invited her to ride along.

He was young, in his late twenties. His appearance was burly and he advertised his poor conditioning by the obesity of his upper body. Still, he was a kind and tender type. He'd recently married. In fact, his wife only two weeks before had their first child; he was faithful to his love and made no advances toward Gyps. To make matters even better, the stranger paid for her meals and let her sleep peacefully in the rear compartment of his truck.

When they arrived in the city, the man knew near nothing about his guest but could tell she was deeply troubled. He invited her to visit his family. He explained that he'd been through tough times and someone had reached out to help him. In his opinion, this stranger had saved his life.

When she refused his offer, he wrote out his name and number and asked Gyps for her contact information. She scribbled Candy Foster on the piece of paper he handed her, and made up a false address as well. The little that she had divulged about herself during the trip was a total fabrication she manufactured on the spot.

When she separated from the trucker, she found herself on the streets of Manhattan. Having never been to New York, and being severely depressed, she walked purposelessly. But as the air began to cool and the sky darkened, it awakened her to the fact that she was alone and without shelter.

Gyps had wisely wandered into a subway station to take advantage of the warmth and cover. She watched as the masses of mankind rapidly exited and entered trains. Then her eye caught sight of a lone male figure wearing a faded, filthy and torn chocolate leather jacket. He walked to the end of the line, far beyond where any of the customers needed to or cared to venture. Then he dropped down to the ground below where the train tracks ran. In an instant, he disappeared.

She might not have given the man another thought except for one fact: as she watched him walking in the opposite direction from where she was standing, she noticed on the back of the jacket in large bold red letters that had lost their luster, the word, HELL. That's when her mind began magically piecing together a series of random and disconnected thoughts, lumping these into a single whole and then employing them—regardless of them being unproven—as facts to be used to issue a verdict.

She was going to hell for her sins. The truck driver had been kind to her only in order to deliver her to the destination where her punishment would be dispensed. The man wearing the jacket had descended in front of her to lead her to her place of suffering, an underground world. Hadn't he glanced back at her, beckoning her to follow, leading her to the land of evil? She had to conclude that he had.

She shuddered at the imagery she had painted since childhood of the godforsaken place, a final destination she sensed from youth she was headed to. There she would meet her fate, an eternity of suffering. The world would turn to fire—bright yellow, red and orange—so hot that her eyes would melt from the heat. She'd gag from trying to breathe the fumes of volcanic-like explosions of gas. The sound of voices would screech so that her ears would fill with the sensation of needles being shoved deep within to the primitive structures of her brain.

Then before even being taken to Satan for the penalty phase of her trial, long passageways filled with giant serpents shooting venom from their fangs would have to be traversed. Her clothing would be pulled off, leaving her naked for the prehistoric dogs to begin gnawing on her flesh.

Then the floor would burn and massive eyes would glare out from the madness around her. Only then would she hear the first intelligible, yet infernal and pan-demonic words, "I am Satan; I am your master. Come, I will show you to your room…"

For Gyps it all seemed real as she jumped off the ramp and down to the level where the trains raced along to pick up passengers lucky enough to be destined for locations other than where she was going. She noticed that once she descended into the dark, that there was a small doorway leading to a stairwell. She followed it downward, level upon level, sure that her deserved discipline was soon to be inflicted.

Finally, she stepped out on to a dirt footing. The ground was cold but not damp or frozen. It was pitch black in some areas but intermittently light filtered through from above, an unanticipated phenomenon for a young lady expecting the worst. Then she saw what she would have thought to be shacks, if they had been in a destitute area of a backward country. For there were what she was sure were walls constructed of everything from cardboard to wood to metal sheeting, the make-shift structures separated by great distance from one another much like pioneers who had staked out parcels of land on a prairie upon which they had built cabins.

She ventured deeper into the world she now realized was one she had heard of, a sad habitat for thousands of homeless making a life for themselves under the New York City subway system. The fact was confirmed as she periodically saw outlines of what she was certain were human beings.

Gyps stood about five-foot seven in height and weighed no more than a hundred and twenty pounds. Her slight figure was well endowed in the areas women typically find most advantageous, and men most appealing. Those elements of her figure were, of course, fixed by nature. But when it came to all of the other ingredients composing her appearance, Gyps in her prior life as a working girl delighted in creating mystery and intrigue.

For example, from week to week the color and style of her hair would change, along with the costumes in which she'd clothe herself. From her imagination, she would invent new roles to enact as well. Thus, her style of speech, manner of gesturing, and tone of voice might alter with the same expertise as a professional impersonator. She was a born actress who never had the opportunity to play a formal part in theater but enjoyed performing on her own the multitude of characters she invented.

The enactment of these transformations would be carried out with such perfection that the men who routinely came to visit her at Misty's would never know what they were going to get from one evening to another. In fact, so skilled was she at modifying her presentation that there were regulars who were surprised when she assured them that indeed she was the same lady they had enjoyed on their prior visit.

All in all, it made her top of the line merchandise at Misty's, in spite of the fact that she was the youngest employee. Now, she was about to play an entirely new role. As she investigated what was to become her new home, she was as attractive as a…vagrant; she hadn't bathed in days, the clothing she wore—her only possessions—were soiled and stank, and her hair was beginning to knot from oils, dirt and neglect of brushing.

After investigating by meandering underground for miles she was exhausted, finally cuddling next to what seemed to her to be the most lavish of the dwellings she'd come across. She fell into a deep sleep immediately. When she awakened she noticed she was hungry. She didn't' have a penny to buy food. Her life as a homeless person was about to begin.

She recognized a human figure moving toward a doorway that was dimly illuminated by a light shining from a train crossing sign above. She followed. She ascended stairs several levels before she exited to what she took for a trap door that opened into an alleyway. She crawled out, taking note of her location so that she could re-enter later. She had found her Hell, the final resting place where she would be rightfully punished. Still, she needed food and water or there would be no Gyps left to pay for her sins.

What does a person do when they possess nothing but the rags on their body? How do they provide themselves with the basic necessities to survive?

Gyps had no idea. While her life up to that point had been no carnival, she had never wanted for nourishing food or a setting within which to live. The underworld was new for her. She needed instruction on how to play her new role as the "street trash" she now envisioned she had become, and would remain for the duration of her self-imposed lifetime sentence.

They say that when the pupil is ready, the teacher will appear. Gyps would have to make it without a map to follow; there would be no tutor. Making matters worse, the kid had her own system of justice and was determined to administer it in a manner leaving her childhood evil dispenser, Satan, seem like a wimp.

CHAPTER 4: 4,018 DAYS IN HELL, AND COUNTING

Who's counting? When you're having a ball, an eon of time wafts past like a fall breeze. Likewise, at the other end of the satisfaction scale, where suffering becomes an inescapable companion, hours, days, weeks, months and years sneak by like slithering thieves in the blackness of night. Gyps had lost track of time on the dark side.

The lady couldn't have planned her choice of lodging better had she stopped in at a realtor's office and asked where would be the most prestigious location to settle. She had roamed the dimness beneath the rail system for several days, near starving, sleeping on the dirt surface and drinking only when she passed a leaking pipe from above her.

Her stomach began to cramp, so much that the pain

reminded her not only of hunger but also fear. The thought of food disgusted her. She might have died of malnutrition had it not been for an indomitable human drive, survival. As much as she tried to clobber the instinct, seeking liberation to allow her vile existence to end, she found she was no challenge to the persuasion of man's fierce will to wake up to face the next hideous day.

She could never recount how long it was before she had finally followed the human figure that had led her to the trap door from which she ventured upward to explore the world of sun, air and…humanity. She did realize that her eyes couldn't focus at first, blinded by the brightness of a clear spring day. She walked through the alley and then turned to her right, where she was swallowed into a street mobbed by people hustling in every direction and at a brisk speed.

Finally she began to make out images and discerned that she had landed in a world of opulence; people were wearing fine clothing and had an air of importance. Then what registered next was a huge sign reading, *Whole Foods*.

Gyps understood that the company existed to turn a profit and wasn't inclined toward altruism. However, she reasoned that somewhere hidden outside the bowels of the store was an area where damaged packages of foods, rotting vegetables and fruits, and returned goods that couldn't be resold were dumped.

She read the city sign that informed her she was at

Columbus Square, on the southwest corner of Central Park. The subway system below was a transition point for the red, orange and blue lines, and below that was her home. She was looking for a charitable side from the cold-hearted retailer.

Within a short time, Gyps had identified where the trucks came to pick up trash. She helped herself to more food than she could imagine eating; the gold prize from the first day of scavenging went to a bag of whole grain rice that had been tossed due to a hole in the packaging. She used an old sack she found in the container to load her provisions.

She then moseyed along 59th Street toward The Hudson River Parkway. During her journey, she found an old sleeping bag along with outdoor cooking gear. She also noticed in a commercial dumpster a long electrical cord, recalling that near where she was sleeping there was a power outlet no doubt used by crews sent down by the transit company to do repairs.

Over the course of the next few weeks, Gyps would build a stockpile of materials that she'd transport in a dilapidated shopping cart to her point of entry to the underground. She then carried the provisions to where she was building her home. Over time from people's trash she'd collected items ranging from an electric frying pan to a small room heater to a wardrobe of clothing articles to a flashlight to grooming aids to a small mattress—all dumped by local residents.

What she lacked the skill or experience to do was build a structure to protect herself or her newfound possessions. She did wisely select a plot of land off from the main walkway and therefore not likely to be discovered by her neighbors. With an inexhaustible supply of nutritious foods, along with warmth and comfort for sleep, she was living a life better than she'd admit deserving.

Not more than a hundred yards from her dwelling was a constantly available water source. The trickling was not going to provide a comfortable shower but with patience, and tolerance of the cold, she was able to routinely wash herself and keep her clothing clean. She was able to groom herself sufficiently so that on excursions into the city, nobody would have had a clue that she was homeless. However, it was of little importance since she never associated with other people.

Her neighborhood was rich in culture, as well as people with money. Occasionally she'd walk to 62nd Street and Columbus Avenue where the New York City Ballet building was located. Other times she'd go to the corner of 64th Street and Amsterdam Avenue to see the Metropolitan Opera House. At those destinations, she'd watch as ticket holders went into and exited performances, the feelings of envy and isolation these experiences would heap on her seemed the perfect remedy for when she was close to forgetting the suffering she deserved.

Then there were times she'd venture further west in this safe Upper West Side area, eventually arriving at the park along the Hudson River. There she'd sit and watch people bicycling along the path while boats would be slowly moving through the waterway. Sometimes a bum or a young person wandering alone on the grass would approach her. Gyps would refuse to engage in conversation. Instead, without a word she'd pick herself up and walk away.

There were many times she wondered if she could still speak. Then she'd test her vocal capability by engaging herself in long dialogues, these discussions usually focused on themes of self-revilement for all the wrongs she had committed in her life. Her only exchanges with other humans were when on a few occasions she'd caused noise while rummaging through someone's trash and received a deserved chastisement, to which she might reflectively respond, "I'm sorry."

What these journeys into the surrounding neighborhoods did do for Gyps was aid her in becoming proficient at finding the wares she needed to live independently, and free of society. So practiced was she after a spell of honing her skills that she was building an inventory of items, many of which she had no need for. As the months, and then years, passed, she had collected a warehouse of supplies. She couldn't explain why, but it was after almost a decade had elapsed of her living the dull and punishing existence being described that she decided she wanted to accumulate a new item, money.

It was then that she began polishing and dusting

some of the more precious items she had run across while canvassing dumpsters and trash containers. Her intent was to sell them. A used iPad brought ten dollars and a working room fan, five. Once she was shocked that an old watch attached to a gold chain she'd found in the filth next to a trash container sold for two hundred dollars at a pawnshop—she later reasoned that the owner of the business had suckered her. Nevertheless, in addition to what she was accumulating from sales she also found coins and an occasional bill lying on the ground.

Early on, she had dug out a small vault in the ground where she deposited the change or paper currency. She had no idea how much she had accumulated since the enterprising spirit had been awakened. Regardless, now yearning to build her fortune she was daily adding to the dirt-dug safe.

Then one afternoon she decided to count everything. With her flashlight, she began pulling out a mass of soiled bills along with pennies, nickels, dimes and quarters, organizing them in groups on her sleeping bag. When she finished, she was shocked to find she had a net worth of $1,453.56.

She took the money and placed it in an old Hermes handbag one of the wealthier residents had lost interest in. Changing clothes, she selected a white short- sleeve top and a pair of sweatpants along with worn tennis shoes. She combed her hair neatly and then tied it in a bun on the top of her head. With her flashlight, she scanned the area she'd called home for a period that now exceeded a decade. Then she switched the light off and tossed it on the sleeping bag.

She turned to leave, whispering to the only person she had carried on a conversation with for what she would soon calculate to be a span of eleven years, herself. "Goodbye," she said softly, recalling that her only communication with the outside world since dissolving into the underground was a single post card.

She had made a solemn pledge to Misty that she would never again make an attempt to contact any of the girls at the ranch. Adding to her sins, she had violated the agreement when she'd written a postcard to Crystal shortly after she arrived in New York—she had no idea why she sent it and in fact never signed it. All it said was, *I love you. I miss you.* She was certain her closest friend at Misty's wouldn't have recognized it was from her in that she'd scribbled such that the script could never be determined to have been by her hand.

Gyps made her way to the street. She had passed the Columbus Square sign thousands of time after coming up from the stench and darkness of the world beneath, but never before stopped to stare into a window of any of the stores. Remarkably, she realized that not once during the entire duration of her retreat from being an active member of society had she looked at herself.

It was on the day she was on her way out of New York that for the first time she set eyes on her image.

Immediately she recognized that her skin was pale and her hair lacked its usual luster. But most astonishing was that she couldn't discern any disdain for the creature eyeing back at her. Was it possible, she wondered, that she had paid for her sins, that what was peering out from the reflection was a subtle, insidious and unconscious signal of expiation? If so, could that be what had motivated her seemingly rash decision to abandon ship? She didn't even know if a parole for having atoned would be something she'd root for.

Gyps went to the New York Penn Station and purchased a ticket to Las Vegas, Nevada. Was she going home? It was scheduled as a three-day bus ride, but after seven years from the time she left New York she was still lost with no intention of being found.

CHAPTER 5: MEANWHILE, BACK AT THE RANCH

While Gyps was making her return to the state of Nevada, her daughter, Star, had passed her eleventh birthday. Gyps herself was twenty-nine. Misty was forty-four. Father Time was in his usual stubbornly merciless mood, tacking on years with a vengeance.

The main room at Misty's was quiet except for a pre-teen girl off to the side rehearsing a speech. Several girls including Crystal, Ricki, Vera, Honey and Toni were serving as an audience. The center of attraction was a slender thing with shiny satin brunette hair combed straight down to the shoulders where it perked up in a natural wave. She was wearing a flesh-colored Lacoste shirt, navy blue short skirt with matching leggings, and a pair of dark purple suede Slouchy Boots.

"I've nursed millions all over the world, dying of

starvation, disease and war. Then I come home to watch shooting and killing in the streets…right where I live," she expressed with theatric outrage. "And you ask me for love! If you can find it, breathing under the smoke and stench of my flesh…" Her words trailed off as if her focus of attention had taken a sedative. "Then I beg you…"she slowly muttered.

Now she stopped, her sweet, childish, serene face that typically would be dimpling her cheeks instead defiantly flattened from irritation. Standing, she lightly tapped her right foot on the floor and raised her arms part way to express the disappointment in herself that she couldn't forgive.

"Wait," she called out to her audience, trying to re-compose for a second attempt. "I'm going to try it one more time. I swear I won't mess it up this time." Star straightened her body and deliberately constructed a costumed smile with her lips. "And you ask for love! If you…"

Again she halted, this time stomping the same foot while gritting her teeth: a second failure was unforgivable.

The upbraiding she had been delivering for her poor performance was interrupted by the sound of three nicely dressed college-aged men entering; their bois-terousness redirected Star's attention. The group related like frat brothers about to conquer a keg of beer. Com-ically, they were standing in a line, angled perfectly at a forty-five degree angle to one another. Simultaneously, they took deep breaths of air as if they had just awakened to the freshness of a mountainous altitude.

"Girls, girls, girls; all for our taking," Ryan heralded to his comrades as if they could now enjoy the fruits of a military victory.

"I don't know a whole lot about living with 'em, but I sure can't live without 'em," Cameron proclaimed, as his eyes were drawn outward by the lusciousness of each of the ladies.

So delirious with the anticipation of pleasure sure to come their way, the threesome paused for a few cheery hand-slaps and inverted shakes.

"Look at that little red head over there," Ryan called out, pointing to Abby, who smiled back at him. "That's going to be my appetizer, boys," he boasted.

"What are you thinking, my good friend? A four-course meal, five courses? What exactly are we looking at?" Cameron aired to Ryan in a most contemplative tone.

"We're lookin' at a feast," Ryan smirked at his buddy. "I'm thinking a medieval, face-stuffing, engorging all-out binge. Gentlemen, are we ready to serve these lovely ladies?"

Misty had been in a meeting when the boys arrived. Their visit had been scheduled: she knew who one of them was, further aware that there would be two companions. She told them to go into the main hall and she'd be there shortly. She entered the room with a fine smile, having overheard their entertaining exhortations.

"I take it you're...Le Madam," Cameron stated.

"I don't believe you men have been here before," Misty responded with a nod to confirm her identity.

"We like to make the rounds, all around town," Cameron giggled, joined by his two friends in what now sounded like three guys not wanting to lose nerve in front of one another.

Misty sensed their cockiness was no more than a transparent shield to obscure their inexperience. She took control of the situation. However, rather than insult their insecurity, she toyed with it.

"I see. So obviously it's not the first time for you men," she complimented.

"No way! Uh...we've—"

Misty interrupted Cameron. "Good, because my girls like experienced men. I'm sure you fellows know that Misty's is not like any of the other joints around here. So if you'll allow me, I'm going to take it upon myself to make sure each of you get...the perfect lady.

"That's fine; I mean all the ladies..." Ryan stopped to examine each in succession. "They all look great."

"Yeah, really. I'll do them all," Cameron blurted out triumphantly.

"Me too," Ryan declared, duplicating his friend's silliness.

"Me three," Justin added, trying to match his associate's confidence but with obvious dubitation.

The girls listening to the encounter couldn't resist a titter. But Ryan and Cameron were not finished. They engaged in a short dialogue, almost as if they had rehearsed a skit.

"Now, we're under the impression that most of your customers are…high-end folk," Ryan addressed Misty.

"Ah, yes," Cameron asserted as if Ryan's statement sparked a past memory. "I believe I recall hearing that."

"Might we say that these men are typically the type who require a good deal of…what should I say, superfluities?" Ryan opined.

"Pampering," Cameron embellished.

"Exactly, my man. But we won't be requesting any sugarcoating. Let me put it plainly, madam, we three wanna skip the love and move right to the lovin'."

"Lots of the lovin'," Cameron reiterated gleefully.

"How about we start off one at a time?" Misty suggested, her eyes squinting as if in a deeply ponderous state; though the truth was that she had been having bouts of severe headaches that would onset randomly, last only a few seconds, and then as mysteriously as they appeared, dissolve. She hadn't mentioned them to anybody but they disturbed her.

"Let's do it!" Cameron elated.

"You men aren't in a hurry, I hope?" Misty queried happily, her head having cleared.

"Tell the ladies we're theirs for all eternity," Ryan swooned.

Misty glanced at her crew. Each was in their own subtle manner now aping their clients.

"It might be best to take it slow and soak it in," Misty grinned but without mocking. "Can I offer you something to drink, to eat…a fine cigar…perhaps a game of pool?"

"You can offer us whatever you want, but there's only one thing we'll take," Ryan answered.

"Okay, I see there's no holding you back."

Misty reached out to grip Ryan's healthy frame by the shoulders, staring directly into his eyes as if studying him.

"You like contact sports, do you?"

"You bet," he responded excitedly.

Misty scanned the room with deliberation. Finally she focused on Ricki, a tall girl with a light complexion and long jet-black hair.

"Ricki," she called out, "this one is all you. Take him to the stable for a ride."

Ricki greeted Ryan with a cute curtsy. Star was still off to the side of the room, but observing. She mimicked Ricki, including the slight bow followed by a handshake. Ricki looped her hand around Ryan's arm and led him out of the room. Misty was already focused on Cameron.

"You…you're not a bad looking kid. What am I going to do about this one?" she posed to herself.

"I'll make it easy on you," Cameron responded. "Call out that girl in the back," he instructed, pointing to Honey, a short stocky but generously and well-proportioned girl with light black skin and short curly black hair. "Throw us in a room and fasten your seatbelt.

"Your wish is my command, sir," Misty said demurely, simultaneously motioning for Honey to come over to the young man who was now smiling while unconsciously rubbing his hands through his head of thick wavy light brown hair.

Honey's eyes glistened coyly as she nodded to Cameron. Then she motioned with her head for him to follow, turning and walking ahead to excite him with her swishing tight butt.

"What's your name?" Misty asked, finally addressing the last and by far quietest of the group.

"Justin," he answered tentatively.

"You look familiar," Misty commented, noticing a connection she couldn't place. "I've seen your picture."

"My father...he's known in these parts."

"Oh, yes, that's it. My God, you're Hugh Crawford's boy."

"Yes, I am," Justin admitted, leaning close to Misty to whisper in her ear a confession more than a disclosure; even if he had in mind the latter he'd have never known he was the son of Misty's partner, nor that he also had a baby half-sister.

The secretive words he did share with Misty drew out

a part of her personality she rarely had the opportunity to employ with a client, a philosophical bent speaking to the intelligence and wisdom of this woman.

"At least you're a man who can think for himself; there aren't many of them, believe it or not, men or women. It seems to me most prefer to let their mind be filled by garbage fed to them by others; if they had an original though it would probably scare them to death."

"I just try to figure out what works for me. I guess I'm looking for a different sort of relationship," Justin answered.

"You just follow that heart of yours and I know you'll find exactly the right thing."

"But listen," Justin addressed Misty in a soft tone. "The guys—"

"I know how it is. This is between you and I...deal?"

Justin gestured appreciation. As he did, for the first time he noticed Star, now resuming practicing her speech in front of a mirror. Misty led him close to where the girl was attempting to get her presentation mastered; she motioned for him to take a seat and then walked off. Star looked over at Justin as Misty left.

"Hey, want to hear a speech I'm working on?"

"Sure."

Star stood straight in front of the mirror, pausing for a few seconds to focus her attention.

"I've nursed millions all over the world dying of starvation, disease and war. Then I come home to watch shooting and killing in the streets…where I live." With a more polished tone of outrage than with prior attempts, she continued. "And you ask me for love! If you can find it, breathing under the smoke and stench of my flesh then I beg you," she entreated, "give me back my life for I fear I have fallen victim to the death of my generation."

She nailed it, relieved and proud that at last she had a perfect reading. The bow she now took—first in front of the mirror and then to Justin as she turned to face him—was deserved.

"Well done," Justin complimented. "Am I supposed to guess what great statesman spoke that?"

"No. I wrote it…well, I wrote half of it. Okay, I didn't write quite that much but I helped Professor Wookie do it in class."

"Where do you go to school?"

"I don't go to a place to learn; my school is here. All of my teachers come to me; literature, music, history, philosophy, science, language…and more language," she frowned. "Misty makes me take Latin, French and Chinese…oh my god, she even has me studying English."

"But what are you doing in a place like this? You live here?"

"Of course. Misty is like my mom; I mean she is my mom because the mom who birthed me died. And all the girls, well, they're not really my sisters but I call them sisters because that's what they're like to me. I have a whole family, just like I guess you do."

"Sisters?"

"Yep. When I was little I always pretended I was in a convent. There was sister Angie, sister Arissa…some of them grew up and left but there's still Honey, Ricki, Crystal, Holly, Cora, Vera, Abby." She stopped to catch her breath after rattling off the names. "I have enough sisters for a football team."

"That's a clever way to imagine it," Justin again praised her.

"Kids always make things up. But now that I'm grown up, I know the truth."

"Isn't it kind of strange? I mean knowing what all the ladies do here?"

"Not at all. Misty's says she training them to be the top professionals in the world."

"I'll bet they already are."

"Then why didn't you meet with one of them? I think you'd like Vera," she suggested, pausing on another thought. "Aren't you stressed?"

"I'm stressed a lot," he admitted. "I don't know… hey, let's talk about something else before I embarrass myself."

"Okay, but they're the best relaxation engineers money can buy," Star assured him.

"Relaxation engineers?" Justin chuckled.

"Do you not even know what we do here?" she posed to him as if he was daffy. "Misty matches you all up with one of my sisters. Then they take you…they tell me they take you to another world, but they never tell me where it is. Anyway, I've seen them take you to a room. Then they talk to you about your problems, give you massages…and everyone leaves relaxed."

"I guess I didn't understand," Justin responded, looking curiously at the misinformed young girl.

"So, you going to come back and try it?"

"I don't know," he answered hesitantly.

"Oh," Star expressed with a hint of disappointment.

Sensing he'd be leaving soon, she held out her hand to shake.

"What's your name?"

"Justin. And yours?"

"I'm Star," she answered, looking unabashedly into the older young man's eyes. "Come on. I'll take you back to Misty."

She reached for his hand and led him away.

"I'll try and come back." He smiled. "Knowing my friends, you can count on it."

CHAPTER 6: BIRTHDAYS AT MISTY'S

It was July 30th again. Misty had put on a big celebration for the little girl who had become the "star" attraction at her place of business. Decorations had been
placed throughout the main room, including, *HAPPY
BIRTHDAY, STAR*, banners. Star was wearing a new
western riding outfit her sisters had bought for her. The
wool tan-colored hat with an orange feather sticking out
of the thin brown band around the crown fell onto her
back, secured by a leather strap draped around her neck.

There were several men sitting at the poker table,
biological dad Hugh Crawford one of them. They had
each been offered a piece of her birthday cake. Star was
spooning her favorite flavor frosting, dark chocolate.

"Finish that cake and you're off to bed, young lady,"
Misty called from the other side of the room.

"It's my birthday," Star protested with a pleading face.

"Tomorrow you have a busy schedule," Misty reminded her, approaching close enough that Star thought she perceived irresolution in her voice.

"But the men want me to help them play cards first."

"You leave the games to them," Misty whispered in her ear, but loud enough that everyone at the table could hear. "You don't want to hang out with those bums any more than you have to," she jested.

"Don't listen to that talk," Hugh smiled. "Come over here and give old Uncle Hugh some help…twelfth birthday, my Lord, time flies."

"Thirteenth," Star corrected with a coy smirk.

"Don't rush it," Hugh advised. "Those years race by all too fast. Enjoy it while you can."

"But it's my thirteenth birthday," Star insisted.

"How do you figure that, my little genius?" Hugh posed.

"The day I was born was the first, then when I turned one it was the second," she continued, numbering each birthday, correctly, one more in total than the celebrated number. "See, it's my thirteenth, unless nobody celebrated the day I was born," she giggled as Hugh tickled her to delight to reward her cleverness.

"Five minutes more, my darling, and it's off to bed for you," Misty assured her with a pump of the head.

"You see, Star," Hugh went on to the business of his

poker hand, "what I'm trying to figure out is if this guy across the table from me is bluffing."

"Bluffing? I think I know what it is."

"Let me make sure, Star, because this is important. Let's say that sweet, innocent looking man over there has the worst cards in the deck. You wouldn't make such a large bet on a miserable hand would you, Luke?" he smirked at his opponent. "Well, Star, if he's put up a lot of money on a lousy hand thinking that he'll scare everyone away and he'll win the pot, that's a bluff." He stopped to contemplate. "My job is to figure out if he's a fake. Think he could be trying to trick me, Star?"

Star made a childish face, indicating she didn't know the answer to his question.

"Come on, Hugh. In or out," Luke insisted while lighting a cigar.

"Hold on there, partner. Let the girl think," Hugh requested, as he turned to address Star. "You see, darlin', usually when a man bluffs he gives it away. He'll do something weird, something that just doesn't look right. That's what to look for. Can you see anything?"

"Yeah, I saw him scratch it," Star roared jubilantly.

"I saw it too, my dear."

Star was so ecstatic she hid her head under the table. The rest of the players were enjoying the childish antics, but not Luke.

"I believe you've been scratching the old stache again, Luke," Hugh declared.

"He has. I saw him do it," Star laughed.

"All right then, Mr. Hotshot," Hugh called out, at the same time nonchalantly taking a piece of cake to his mouth. "I'll have to raise you."

Luke took his cards and tossed them on the table, defeated.

"I got me a deuce and seven in the hole, boys, and she's all mine," Hugh bragged, referring both to his bluffing the bluff as well as to Star's hand-winning observation.

Star hopped off Hugh's lap and went to the other side of the room. She was pouring a glass of water when a middle-aged man, Conrad, approached her. The size of the room permitted his encounter to go unheard, except by Star.

"That's a hot get-up you have on, sweet thing."

"My sisters gave it to me for my birthday," Star answered innocently. "And Misty gave me a real pony to go with it. I named him, Pilot. I'll show him to you if you like horses."

"There's lots of things I'd like you to show me," Conrad said crudely. "You know, you're getting to be quite a lady. Are you working yet?" he chuckled.

"You mean like my sisters in relaxation?"

"Exactly," he noted with a sinister smile.

"Oh, no. I have to learn the methods first."

"I'll bet I'd like your methods just fine," he expressed vulgarly, while he reached out and ran his hand across

Star's chest. "I'd like to show you how much fun it is to touch."

"Oh, Mr. Conrad," Star reacted by jumping backward, her vocal tone elevated. "I don't think you should do that."

Star quickly ran off, leaving Conrad smiling delightfully. By chance, however, both Hugh and Misty had witnessed the latter part of the exchange, with Conrad touching her. Hugh aggressively stood up but Misty put her arm out to stop him.

"Goddamn it! Let me handle this, Hugh."

"Misty, it's my—"

"Exactly. I'll urge you to leave it alone."

Misty raced over to Conrad who was still standing by himself. She grabbed his arm and swung him around, just as two security men were approaching.

"What the hell's going on here?" she screeched. "That is MY daughter; she's a child."

By now Misty had attracted the attention of about everyone in the main room, several of the girls encircling Misty and Conrad.

"Look yourself," Conrad slurred, clearly inebriated. "She's more than a child. And this is a damn whorehouse; I thought we get to choose."

"You're out of here; don't ever come back," Misty ordered, but with restraint.

She motioned for her staff to escort him from the

ranch. Conrad only offered a defiant shrug as he sauntered toward the exit.

Misty looked across the room and saw Star being entertained by some of the men so as to distract her from the hostility. She sat down for a moment, appearing out of breath—in truth the stress of the moment might have been the precipitating event causing another of the ever more frequent brief episodes of head pain.

Hugh approached her with a concerned look on his face. "Misty, are you well?"

"Of course. Why do you ask?"

"You looked as if you were in pain."

"It's nothing. Once in a while I get these spells. You know how it is," she replied in a dismissive tone, as she stood upright.

The physical pain having passed, she used the occasion to confront Hugh about something that was bothering her. It was his impulsive reaction to the Conrad incident, his protectiveness toward Star, as well as a few comments he'd made more recently that indicated he had more interest in Star's life than Misty wanted. "I don't want you to ever take that much of a role in public with Star again," she admonished.

"She is mine. You know things can change in the future," Hugh replied, the vagueness of his words validating to Misty that she would likely be dealing with a breach of their prior agreement sooner rather than... never.

"You just check that, Hugh. As far as you're concerned, there is no future."

Misty's sharp words coincided with her taking off to be with Star. Conrad had left. Misty motioned across the room for Star to come to her. When she did, Misty took her by the arm and led her to the child's bedroom. She motioned for Star to sit, insisted she listen to her melodic lecture that when over might have been entitled, *Bums*.

"Now you listen to me, Star. Considering what just happened, I think it's time we talk about men," Misty began her short but poignant speech. "Men, they can be great up to a point…but when it comes down to it, they all got a bag of dirty tricks. You'll learn that they all got these smilin' eyes, that'll drop you down to the tip of demise. Sure, they can be kind as can be; they can suit you fine for a while you see, but don't never let 'em ever too close to you, hun…well, I'll tell you why, they're all bums. Not me. I ain't no sucker, they can play those games on another one brother, give me something better than another bum." She stopped to embrace Star. "I'm so sorry that had to happen to you, my love."

"Misty, is this," Star paused to look directly into Misty's eyes as she mimicked Conrad's words, "a damn whorehouse?"

Misty stood speechless for several seconds, digesting a discussion she knew she would eventually be called upon to have with the girl.

"We'll talk more later. How's that?"

"It is, huh? What does that make you? You're not a…
prostitute, are you?"

"No," Misty smiled, "I've never been close to being
one. They call me the madam. Star, this is my business.
I'm no different than any other president, general man-
ager or CEO who runs an enterprise."

"I played dumb, but I've known the truth about my
sisters for a long time."

"Don't lose respect for them, that's what's most important. They're all doing what they can to improve
their lives. Honey, they didn't have the chance to learn
like you when they were your age," she explained while
holding Star by the shoulders to face her. "Now I'll share
a secret with you. Your sisters, they have better lives
than most women in the world dream about. They'll be
independent financially when they retire too."

"How?"

"Later, Star. You need to go to bed. Now remember,
respect them, every one of them. They deserve it…and
they love you."

"I love them too," Star affirmed with weepy eyes.

Star couldn't fall asleep for over an hour. She experienced no trauma from the perverse solicitation by Conrad. What kept Star up was mystery and imagination.
She had noticed for some time that subtle changes were
taking place in her body. Everybody in her world delighted in her as the "little girl," a role she deliberately

played for the entertainment of the people she loved. But more recently she sensed and felt the woman within her peeking out, engaging in a game of hide and seek. The emerging self was unable to find places where Star couldn't find it.

She wondered what it would be like to be touched, even experimented privately on occasion with manipulating herself, something she discovered while reading on the internet. She found it satisfying. Then while she lay in the dark, she rehearsed the words Misty had sung to her. "...don't never let 'em ever too close to you, hun...well, I'll tell you why, they are all bums."

Did Misty not like men? When she thought about it, she realized that she'd never known Misty to have a friend, male or female, though she did notice that Misty related different with Hugh than any of the other guests coming to the ranch.

The thoughts were now moving through her mind like figures riding up and down on escalators. She never saw Hugh take off with any of her sisters. He'd come to play cards and chat with Misty, spend a lot of time paying attention to her, but then he'd leave. As she dwelled more on the subject of Hugh, she recognized that his interest in her was much greater than anyone else who came to Misty's, almost as if his arrival at Misty's was motivated by wanting to see little Star.

She finally drifted off. When she woke up she laid in the dark, the thin strands of light outlining the perimeter

of the windows alerting her that it was a bright morning. She knew that soon she'd receive visitors coming to
wake her up.

But she was deliberating a dream. It wouldn't go
away, the remnants coating her first consciousness of
the day. It seemed she was being ordered to take possession of the imagery before she'd be permitted to address
her daily responsibilities. Thus, she relived as much of
the sleep experience as she could.

In her dream, she recalled that she was reading a
book. There were pictures, mostly of humans but she
couldn't recognize any of them. She had the impression
that somebody was in the room with her though whom-
ever it was she couldn't see and when she'd ask a question the person accompanying her wouldn't answer.

She remembered that several times she threw down
the book, angered about something but not being able
to figure out what was annoying her. Then, in spite of
the irritation she was experiencing, each time she felt
a compulsion to pick it up again and attempt to read
it. She noticed as she tried to peruse the script that the
letters would change such that in an instant it might go
from French to English to Latin. Then, no matter how
hard she stared at the letters, she couldn't make out a
single word.

Making the interpretation more distressing was the
fact that the iterations of her attempting to comprehend
what she was experiencing resulted in the transformation

between languages occurring faster and faster while the pictures became increasingly more obscure, to where they seemed to blend into a single stream of incoherence. Several times she tried shouting to the individual she believed to be with her. She was attempting to cry out for help, but she couldn't produce a sound. It seemed to Star that the dream went on for an eternity.

As she tried to dissect it that next morning while in bed, she had only one insight but it was a rather brilliant one. Every picture represented a person who was part of her life and the words underneath were pieces of their story, the bigger picture a tale of who Star was and where she came from. For as she performed her surgical analysis, she recognized that the exasperation she went through while asleep was not much different than what she endured more frequently in her waking life.

Star knew one or more vital pieces of data were missing. She was happy. She was loved. She had no need that went unfulfilled. But…she had questions. Then when she posed them, nobody answered. She sensed evasiveness on the part of Misty. In fact, the few times she tried to bring up the topic of her mother, the inquiry earned no more than a quick dismissal, Misty's attitude suggested to Star that there was something shameful about the woman who gave birth to her. Even her sisters, if they knew anything about Star's mother, refused to venture into a discussion about the woman. Regarding her father, she was told simply that nobody knew who he was.

The book in her dream, she surmised, was the yarn of her life being told in symbols she couldn't interpret—her history was a mystery, filled with discrete elements about which she couldn't determine the interrelatedness or lack thereof. It had always been that way, confounding. When during the course of her daily existence she butted up to obstacles that were denying her comprehension, her experience would become one of infuriation, exactly as she had experienced in her sleep state.

She had thought about a more serious confrontation with Misty, but each time backed away. It wasn't fear. Rather, she recognized the impulse to retreat motivated by pity. Her experience had been that even approaching the subject casually caused Misty to be uneasy. She'd then feel guilty at the thought of having hurt the only mother she knew.

She'd reached the same dead end of no tangible insights innumerable times in the past, as she did the morning of her dream. Each occasion left her in a funk. She was about to shelve her thoughts when there was a knock on her door.

"Come in," she voiced to whichever of her sisters had been assigned to help her start her day.

It was both Crystal and Honey. Honey went immediately to the window shades to draw them up. Star's room faced easterly and the rays of the morning sun were already intense enough to cause the girl to use her hands to cover her eyes.

"Nine in the morning? Is the little princess ready to rise?" Crystal teased.

"I was just laying here thinking," Star mentioned, knowing she wasn't ready to share the contents of the dream or her limited interpretation.

"Oh, were you? Well, if you were thinking about Conrad, I promise you he's gone for good," Crystal informed her.

"Why was he interested in me? Why didn't he want one of you?"

"*That* is a good question. Let me know when you figure it out."

"Maybe you're too old for his taste, Crystal."

"Maybe *you're* too dull for a beautiful day like today," Honey lightly admonished her sour mood. "I'm depressed just looking at you. Do me a favor and smile for a change. Let Mr. Sun lighten all those heavy burdens you're hauling around."

Star shrugged defiantly, resisting Honey's attempt to lift her sad tone. Honey wasn't in the mood to relent.

"What would it take for me to get a smile out of that face? Am I going to have to squeeze it out myself? Crystal, hold her down."

Crystal gently took her shoulders and pinned them to the mattress, the girl offering no resistance. Then Honey jumped on the bed, mounting Star's body with hers while using her hands to mold her friend's face.

"Let's see. I'll just spread these cheeks as wide as they

go. And, I'll get these little lips stretched out nice and thin," Honey played lovingly.

She paused long enough to examine her work, keeping her hands in place.

"Oh, right, the eye will have to open up a good inch or so. And I may as well perk up that nose while I'm at it," again leaning backward to inspect how the project was coming along. "Nope, I'm absolutely certain that nine out of ten doctors would agree…that's no smile. You're going to have to help me out, my dear."

Star still refused to join in the fun, instead lying passively. As a final attempt to bring her out of her slumber, both Honey and Crystal began speaking to her in rhyme, alternating verses.

"If you frown too long, 'cause you're down too long and you lay around impounded in the ground too long—"

"Then your jaw congeals and locks a bit, your cheeks cement like blocks a bit, and soon enough you're tryin' for a mile to make a smile but that old cold frozen face just doesn't buckle when you need to chuckle—"

"And if you bum too long 'cause you're glum too long and you spend a ton of time feelin' numb too long—"

"Then your eyes'll start to bag a bit, your lips'll start to sag a bit and soon enough you're fightin' for a giggle or a grin—"

They finished the fun off together. "But that lousy

stinkin', drowsy sinkin', stale frail icy face just doesn't jiggle when you wriggle a wiggle with a waggle."

At last the girl submitted, bursting out with laughter. Just then one of the other girls, Toni, stopped by.

"You better get yourself going before Misty finds you loafing. Mr. Crow will be here for your piano lesson at noon and then Mr. Know-It-All, Molliere, is coming for dance."

"Let me ask you something," Star posed with her most adult tone to all three of her sisters.

Recognizing the little one was about to amuse them with a big grown up question they collectively saluted her.

"Yes, sir. At your service," they responded with perfect harmony.

"What's it like?"

"What is what like?" Crystal repeated the question back to her.

"Doing it."

"Okay, honey. What's it like?" Honey stuttered. "What's it like? It's like stealing your big sister's make up and clothes, and sneaking off to try them on before she finds out. It's like…"

"Forget it; I'm just going to have to see for myself," Star declared.

"I think you have time to get out of that bed and get ready for the day first."

"I have another question before I do," Star protested. "What about Misty? I want the truth."

"What about her? Honey inquired.

"She told me she never was one. Well, was she?"

"A prostitute?" Honey giggled. "Never, darlin'. She's smart and tough as they come but she'd never make it in our field. No, she's just running a business."

Star jumped out of bed to present the next question.

"And my mother...was she one?"

"We don't know much about her—"Crystal began to respond before being interrupted.

"It's best that you ask Misty about her." Ricki, who had just entered the room, answered abruptly.

"Well, I might just take up the trade myself."

The girls began laughing at what they knew was a foolish thought. In the meantime, they were starting to get Star ready for the day. Ricki went to her closet and selected clothing, slipping a dress over her head. In her hand Honey was holding a brush and began grooming Star's hair. Crystal pulled a small container of rouge out of her pocket and treated Star to a light application on her cheeks.

"Go on, get your shoes on," Ricki ordered as she handed her a pair of satin pumps.

"Even if you end up sticking around here your whole life, you'll never work like we do. But you could end up running Misty's," Ricki surmised. "You just keep studying."

"I see, I can't be a prostitute but I can sell one," the precocious one concluded. "Well, I'm not interested. I never want to do what Misty does. She just walks around all day talking to people and doing paper work."

"Do you know why it seems so simple?" Crystal posed to her.

"Why?"

"Because she does it so naturally. You can't even tell how hard it is but I know it's not easy. Being a madam is like being an architect, builder, painter and plumber… all rolled into one. Misty sets the tone for everything that happens here. Men forget everything, even the reason they came.

"Our customers come here and do what most people would call sinful or dirty, but Misty found a way for them to feel proud of it. She could have run any business, but this is the one she's a genius at," Crystal explained near reverently.

Ricki was finishing applying a thin layer of orange-colored lipstick to match her pumps. Then she picked up a small mirror sitting on a dresser, holding it up to Star's face. Looking at herself with make-up thrilled the girl; she bounced around the room.

"And I'm predicting you're going to be as good as Misty at whatever you do," Honey added to the morning pep talk, knowing that many times she'd heard Misty make off-handed comments to the effect that she envisioned Star following in her footsteps. "You just may be the next Misty. After all, name me one other person in the world who has grown up their whole life watching the best of the best take care of business?"

"Well, I'm just not interested in following in her footsteps," Star countered playfully, spinning her little body until she was dizzy. "I wanna be an actress not a sex salesperson, and I don't see any way to do both." Star stopped and a second later produced a devilish grin. "Unless..."

Star stopped again. She positioned herself in front of her small audience, making sure she had their full attention.

"Unless...are you ready? Try this, ladies," she announced adult-like, flawlessly portraying a New Yorker's Jewish accent. "Oh, Mr. James, have I got a deal for you." She pointed to Ricki. "She's getting a little old but I'll touch up the gray, throw on some make up... and okay, okay, a twenty percent discount just for you," she bellowed. "With dinner and drinks on the house... you're killin' me...just this once because you're a special customer."

Star turned away from the girls, a sign intended to notify them that she was about to begin a new scene. By the time she revolved a half-circle to look back at them, her persona was altered. She assumed a sweet western sounding voice, speaking fast-paced like a television pitchman.

"Hi, I'm Star. I'm inviting u'all to come visit me this

weekend at *Misty's Ranch*. Take a look at my inventory," Star said boastfully pointing to Crystal. "This sweet little all-white model comes fully loaded with an oversized duel front end..." She pauses to point at Crystal's breasts. "Hell, look for yourself. And any of you fellows looking for a pickup?" Star hawked, now motioning to Ricki. "Then just climb in this buggy and I guarantee she'll have you doing zero to sixty in under a heartbeat.

"I've got a whoreho...whoops, I've got a whole house full of beauties like these just waiting for you. This weekend, would you rather have a heart attack from feuding with your wife or girlfriend, or from having one of these babies rev up your motor?"

She stopped to scan the audience, three ladies loving the little star. "How's that for a madam?" Star howled.

"Make fun all you like, but you may find you like being a madam more than you can think," Ricki smiled first toward Star and then to the other girls. "Who knows, it may be all that you've been dreaming for."

Star stared blankly as the girls promoted their position.

"My madam," Crystal murmured. "I can see it. We'll all abide by you...we'll step aside for you. You'll be the madam, forever more. You'll be a star, and even more. As the lady said, it might be all you've been dreaming for."

"You'll learn to charm the boys; you'll pick up all our plays," Honey added to the equation. "It's best to profess, that from this very day you won't have it no other way. Star, you'll be our queen, forever more; is it all you've been dreaming for?"

The girls were rejoicing from their impromptu presentation.

"Well, I can be the first girl in the world who has ever dreamed of...Madamland?" Star clowned.

"You can also be the first girl in the world to be punished by Misty for missing your lessons," Ricki warned, realizing they may all be in the soup if they didn't have Star ready for her classes.

The girls left Star to finish preparing for breakfast and then meeting with her teachers. Her spirits had been lifted by the morning play with her sisters. But she still couldn't ditch the gloomy residue from her dream. None of her questions had been answered. If anything, her mind seemed more jumbled.

She felt an unprecedented anger toward Misty. Why? She couldn't express it. It was a vague sensation, as if at least one of the pictures in the dream had to be Misty, and further that if her surrogate mother chose to, she could give names to all the characters and read the words beneath each on the pages.

She had thought of talking to Mr. Crow, her piano teacher. He was the youngest of her instructors, a thin, frail man who had a perceived sensitivity she found missing in most of the men she encountered. He generally began the lesson talking to Star, allowing her to prattle freely about whatever was on her mind. It was an opportunity for her to vent about the heavy demands Misty placed on her time.

Occasionally she'd use it as an opportunity to complain about the difficulty she might be having with another of her professors. But she'd never used those moments to talk about herself and how she felt or what she was thinking. In fact, she realized as she contemplated raising the topic of her dream with Mr. Crow, that she rarely expressed words pertaining to her inner self to anyone.

When she welcomed her teacher in the manner she was trained by Misty, with a slight bow, she was determined to ask his advice. But almost immediately upon seeing him she lost courage, never making the attempt to share the concerns that were conflicting her. Of course, she loved Misty, the woman was as devoted a mother as any child could imagine, but she shuttered at the thought that she detested her at times as well.

There was one other thought she kept hidden in her heart, one she never would have considered discussing with Mr. Crow, or for that matter with anyone. It was the one item in the dream she was sure of, the single image she did finally make out after dwelling on the experience that morning. The last picture was of a man, in her mind certainly not a grown man, but no longer a boy either.

His appearance came to a sharp and clear resolution; he seemed eager to step out of the fog that shrouded the other pictures. Plus, he refused to dissolve like the rest of the images. He presented with thick black-rimmed glasses and she noticed as he was smiling that he looked childishly unsure of himself. He wore a black V-neck sweater unevenly over a white t-shirt, the slightly disheveled look increased his allure to Star: it represented to her that he had cerebral preoccupations that superseded the common superficialities dominating the thinking of most young people. She especially loved his hair. It was sandy blond, straight and cut about two inches in length at the top. She noticed it sprouted naturally upward, seeming to be stretching after having just awakened from a nap.

Would he reappear in another of her dreams soon... or ever? Would she discover him in real life and would he then be the special one she could share the privacy of her person with? These were the questions fouling up her attention as Mr. Crow was instructing her on how to identify *intervals* in the *C Major scale*. Her teacher didn't know it yet, nor for that matter could Star put a label on it, but for the first time it was hormones that were dancing her fingers along 88 keys.

CHAPTER 7: COULD IT BE...LOVE?

It had been about two weeks since her dream. The entire experience, including the stimulating image of the young man, had departed her conscious memory. The constant demands on her time as a result of the rigorous educational program set by Misty ate away at her imagination insidiously like an infestation of termites; rarely was there a moment to journey inside what she was beginning to recognize as a mental gymnasium filled with equipment vital to her development as a budding adult.

Then one afternoon, she had two hours free. She asked Misty for permission to take Pilot for a ride.

"It's fine with me. Just be careful," Misty admonished. "Before you go, can you straighten up the tack room?"

"Of course," Star answered, repressing the ire she had for receiving a conditional approval.

It only took a few minutes to fold the stable blankets and saddle pads, and hang the bits and halters. She was about to organize the collection of Western boots when she was shocked by an interloping voice.

"Hey!"

Star glanced toward the door. The resemblance was unmistakable. His presence re-flamed the passion she had after laboring to bring back that lone image of her past dream, the one she now realized had occurred just after meeting Justin while practicing her speech.

"You scared me."

"Misty told me I could find you here," Justin laughed.

"Once again not interested in one of our fine ladies like your friends?" Star teased.

"I'm feeling relaxed already."

"I know what really goes on here," Star stated matter-a-fact. "You don't have to lie anymore. Hey, I'm free for a couple hours. Want to do something?"

"Anything. Just keep me off a horse," Justin chuckled.

"You came to a brothel that's on a ranch; you can't avoid both the women and the horses."

"I've never been on a horse."

"Never been on a horse!?" she japed. "Today I'll give you your first lesson."

"I'm gonna look stupid."

"It's easy,"

In the corner of the room was a fancy mechanical

practice horse. Star swung it around and pulled it into the center of the room.

"How do you like this baby?"

"My god, it looks real."

"We call him, Horace. Mr. Wozinowietz taught me on him. Looks like a real horse, doesn't he? The best part is once you're up on him, how you move your butt, legs, and hands impact Horace's movement. Come on," she encouraged. "I'll get some boots for you and you'll try."

"Okay, but I don't see myself as a horseman."

"Size nine, right?" she said as she tossed a pair of boots to him, ignoring his skepticism. "Take them with you to practice. You can bring them back the next time you come here and wimp out."

"Very funny," he retorted while slipping on the boots that fit perfectly.

"Okay, let's see if you've got as much guts as this animal. Now, put your left foot here and then...pull yourself up. That's it, nothing to it, right?" she complimented as Justin sat atop the full-sized replica of a stallion. "Listen carefully. First it's about getting used to the motion of the horse. You have to learn to move with the action of his stride. Ready?"

Star took the remote control and aimed it at the animal. It began moving in a rhythmic pattern, bouncing Justin up and down.

"Use your knees and legs to lift your butt off the saddle," she instructed.

Justin wasn't getting it. Instead he was being tumbled around like laundry in a dryer. Star was shooting commands at him but he was being shaken so heavily that he couldn't follow her orders. He finally raised his right arm and called for her to stop the machine. Star pointed the remote and instantaneously the horse came to a halt, nearly landing Justin on the ground.

"The girls inside would have taken it easier on me," he panted.

"You don't listen," she chastised like a frustrated parent. "I told you the horse has a rhythm and you have to go with it; you're fighting it. Now try again," she insisted.

She switched on the machine, but with identical results. Justin was immediately out of control, bouncing on the saddle. Star was exhorting him to try one maneuver after another but he didn't follow her instructions. Realizing the impossibility of the situation, Star's mild reprove of him quickly graduated to zany humor.

"Right you are. I don't think you're going to be rodeo material."

"I thought this was a horse, not a bronco," Justin jested, his words flying as chaotically as his body.

"You're not too quick a learner, my friend," she bellowed as she brought the horse to a slow motion. She was beginning to enjoy what was becoming an increasingly comical situation. "Try one more time. Here, we'll take it real slow."

The horse was hardly moving and Justin took a peaceful deep breath.

"Ready now?" she questioned with a wide, devilish grin.

Gradually she ramped up the speed of the machine, Justin being thrust up and down more violently than even at the beginning.

"You're the worst teacher I could ever imagine," he cried out, unable to restrain his laughter.

Carried away with the game, Star began pushing more buttons, the horse accelerating in speed and intensifying in movement. Star by now was howling gleefully as she watched Justin flying freely atop the training apparatus.

"Say it again," she taunted. "So, I'm the worst teacher?" she queried, pointing the clicker and again raising the speed.

"I can't," Justin sputtered, intentionally breaking up his words to play along with the game.

Worked into a state of ecstasy, Star finally pushed one more button. The horse came to such an abrupt halt it nearly threw Justin forward over its head. By now both Justin and Star were laughing hysterically.

"I know some people who like to pull wings off butterflies. I'll introduce you. I think you'd get along splendidly."

"It's not my fault you can't learn to flow with the simple motion of an animal. My, it's not even a real horse."

She stopped to inspect the man she now was sure had a lead role in the dream episode that had been lying dormant in her mind.

"I think I can summarize you in lyrics. Absolutely, *You Stand Alone*, my friend. And let me tell you, I've seen a few that ain't so prone, but my friend, you stand alone." Justin was about to reply but she silenced him with a wave of her hand. "All my life, I thought I'd known the lowest heights that man could roam, but then you came and my mind was blown, cause my good friend, you stand alone." Star pranced around the room for a moment, trying to control her laughter. "I couldn't find a slower kind…you're all alone!"

"Well, I'm not gonna argue with everything you said. It's not all wrong," Justin finally responded in a manner that might have left Star with the impression that he thought he was in a stage production. "I know you're teasin', but when it comes to reason, or anything like thinkin', you got me honed, I stand alone. And if you're talkin' sense, you're really not too dense, cause you made it known I stand alone."

Justin draped his arm over the neck of the horse, smiling boldly at Star. "If I may continue…I know you're tryin', but when it comes to wit, I'm just a bit too fit, and if you're talking bright, you're right I'm out of sight… you're the one who made it known, I stand alone."

The impromptu dialogue they were crafting was destined for a dual. Neither Star nor Jason were about to be outdone, each of them facing the other as they spoke lines on top of one another.

"Oh, my," Star lead with a tone of feigned indignation," you must be a whole new breed; indeed, you stand alone."

"Indeed! I do. And I'm the only one who's thinkin' sensibly...that is a whole new breed."

"Huh, and I'm the only one who's seein' things in key."

The twosome stood, locked in comedic poses. It was Star who finally broke the glorious silence.

"Well, your friends should be down soon."

"Right," he answered, slightly flustered. "As you can see, we'll never get along. But still, you ought to come out with us one time." Justin paused, carefully inspecting her as if she were a puzzle. "How old are you?"

"Twelve."

"Really?" His mouth was agape. "I'd have thought at least sixteen."

He was right. The young girl practicing her speech during his first visit to Misty's had dashed out of childhood, leaving all her belongings behind; she had no intent of returning. There was no sense mourning over losses that couldn't be replaced and she had sensed for some time that she would have to part with her youth, which she had done like a quick change artist.

So when she awakened one morning to distinct changes in her anatomy, it was not a surprise. She had been awaiting her entry to womanhood, impatient for its arrival. Fortunately for her, it came on like a torrential rain. The tone of her voice altered in a matter of days, to the point where hearing her own speech mystified her in that she couldn't believe it was Star uttering the sounds of a maturing woman.

Her body curved and shaped almost overnight. In fact, it was not only before going to bed that she would carefully inspect her body image; it was every time she had the opportunity to disrobe.

It was more than the physical presentation and vocalization presented to the outside world that announced the birth of adulthood. She was shedding her old coat like a reptile, her sweet, innocent little girl persona was being exchanged for the thoughtful, mature and disciplined garment she was weaving to wear for the remainder of her life.

Justin had rightly dismissed the juvenile he first met. She was a child living in a world of fantasy and innocence, believing that prostitutes were relaxation engineers. But what he couldn't overlook, even while Star was delirious in toying with him on the horse, was that behind the playfulness of her prank, lust was posting riddles to intrigue him.

"Well, twelve is all you get. But you can still be my pupil." She was cleverly attempting to erase an obstacle she knew could not be removed except had she employed deceit, a tactic she would have never permitted.

"Don't your friends look a lot younger than you?"

Justin asked, fishing for an excuse that might permit him to carry on a relationship with this enigmatic girl with whom he sensed a kinship.

"I don't really have friends like most people my age," she informed him. "I know it may sound odd to you, but I don't really have a problem with it; well, to tell you the truth, I've never left Misty's Ranch...ever."

"In your whole life?"

"Everything I could imagine is right here."

"What about other people, other countries...other experience...like going off to college? I'm going away to university myself in a month; I can't wait."

"Someday I'll do it all," she responded wistfully.

"Your life is now. Star," he implored more strongly than he realized, "you can't wait for...someday."

"I know. I'm thinking about it," she answered carelessly.

"Does Misty think you should leave?"

Justin was determined to keep the line of inquiry going, shocked by what he was hearing.

"She's never mentioned it."

At that precise moment, Misty walked into the room.

"I told your buddies you were finishing up. Come on, you better get going," Misty instructed.

Justin waved goodbye to Star, examining her with even greater curiosity. After he left, Misty was alone with Star.

"There's a fine young man; one of the only ones I've

91

seen in a long time," Misty complimented. "I'll be back later."

Misty left the tack room, speaking softly to herself: "Aunt Misty, watching brother and sister at play; what a wonderful sight," she jested. "Who would ever believe it?"

The more apropos question might have been, Will anyone ever suspect it?

There was no reason Star would have. There were no clues for Justin to entertain the thought. Still, a spell had been cast on both of the siblings. If fate would be kind to them it would never be lifted—but destiny's wand waves wildly, educating mankind to the wastefulness of wishing.

CHAPTER 8: ONE SIMPLE QUESTION

Self-imposed or otherwise, Gyps sensed she had been released after a lengthy imprisonment. The social skills that she possessed in a prior life seemed dusty and remote. They resembled remnants she lacked the confidence she could recover. During the days she rode on the bus, she watched as cars and trucks flew by like cosmic debris, her mind urgently rummaged through infinity in search of a finite address from which she could begin comprehending a world she had been banished from for more than a decade.

Over ten years and she'd hardly shared a word with another human soul. Would she have anything worthy of saying now? Would she know how to express it if she did? Was there anyone in the entire world that would care to hear her words? While isolated from her fellow man it had become simple, tolerable...even comfortable. There was nobody to hurt or to disappoint, expectations were non-existent, and any pains experienced on her own part were self-inflicted.

When the driver pulled into the station in Chicago for a stopover, she exited to buy provisions for the remainder of the journey. She had groomed herself well before leaving, even sprayed herself with the remains of a bottle of cologne she collected from a trash container on 64th Street in New York. The dainty fragrance was named Juicy Couture for Women, the aroma one Gyps would have bought for herself when she was working.

While standing in line to purchase a sandwich, there was a man in his mid-thirties in front of her. He turned around and she noticed he was an attractive male, just the type she enjoyed pacifying sexually when she was being paid for delivering thrills. She noticed him draw in an exaggerated breath of air, cocking his head to signal that his olfactory sense was in service.

"Juicy Couture," he smiled, raising the index finger of his right hand to celebrate his accuracy in identifying the scent.

Gyps noticed the muscles in her neck and jaw flex, gripping so tightly she couldn't have moved her mouth had she tried, which was precisely what she didn't want to do. She stared for a second at his pleasant and friendly face before rushing back into the bus, forfeiting the meal she planned to take with her.

Sitting in her seat, she noticed that she was sweating and panting. She had a small mirror in her purse and glanced at the image it projected. She was still beautiful. Even she could see it. All those years of neglect and not a thimble of allure or sensual attraction had been subtracted; if she had to she could still work, she recalled telling herself while she wept before taking the vial of cologne out of her travel case and pouring the remains out the window.

The realization that she couldn't respond back to the man terrified her. The childish act of tossing out the fragrance was her only defense against overwhelming shame; it was also an expression of anger. Worse still, the bitter gesture elicited a deep sense of grief; intentionally getting rid of the fragrance brought back to her how she acquired the designer perfume.

Several months before leaving New York she was walking on West 67th Street, passing a tiny shop, *Alice's Tea Cup*. It was a cute café with a yellow façade and a dark purple awning. She chose to walk on this particular street often because she experienced a peculiarly satisfying sensation whenever she passed in front of the store. To the side was a grey cement stairway leading to a door opening to the several flats located on the two stories above the business.

One afternoon a woman, who Gyps estimated to be about thirty years of age had just opened the door and was about to walk down to the street. Gyps, as she always did when scavenging for junk, had her head down in a sorrowful and shameful pose. But on this occasion, she looked up at the woman and their eyes met, the glance lasting an unusually long time. She remembers the woman having a slight figure and wearing a hot pink tank top, royal blue pants cut short at the ankle and a pair of powder blue tennis shoes. Her hair was jet black, cut very short but with a classy styling.

It wasn't until the woman smiled at Gyps that she put her head back down and walked away. She did notice a small plastic sack the woman was holding in her right hand, remarkable because it was orange in color and the words, *Siela's Italian Market*, were printed in white.

After walking the few blocks to the Hudson River, she turned around and made her way back to where she had seen the woman. That's when she noticed that the bag the lady had been carrying had been placed so it was sitting on the top of the trash container located to the right of the stairwell.

Gyps took what she presumed were scraps left from a meal, not looking at the items until back at her home. She was puzzled by the contents. The trash container was stuffed with fresh packages of food that had never been opened. Then, when she'd make her rounds in the neighborhood about the same time every few days, there would almost without fail be a present waiting. She was sure the same woman was leaving them for her but she wouldn't have had the courage to confront the stranger.

A peculiar sensation came over her as she rehearsed the incidences, first pertaining to the generous woman and then the friendly male who correctly guessed her cologne. Shortly, she was able to attach words to match the disgusting feelings she was trying to avoid owning: selfishness and insensitivity. She despised what had become of her. So wrapped up in self-contempt and pity, she had become a cold, hard creature inflicting human suffering on anyone coming in contact with her.

Yet even with this grand insight she was stumped. Had she willed with all her power to engage these people with a kind gesture or expression of appreciation, a simple human display of giving, she couldn't. In fact, it was that recognition that brought the emotional pain she had suffered all those years to yet a new and greater level of hurt. Gyps realized she was no longer a person; she had lost more than any human could endure, her sense of self. As the reality of her circumstance sunk in, she perceived it similar to a death trap; a suicidal noose was gradually squeezing the last gasps of air from her sick being.

The shattered lady picked herself up and again exited the bus. She walked out of the station and wandered. She headed north to W. Van Buren Street and then went east to S. Canal Street. Then she turned right and went south to W. Polk Street. Again she turned right and walked to

S. Halsted Street, after which she turned right one more time before heading north, landing her a second time at the corner of Halsted and W. Van Buren Streets.

Four right turns, leading her along a rectangular path, one she repeated until out of exhaustion she fell over, not able to move until the next morning. She was blessed not to have in her possession a means of self-destruction; the break of day was so unendurably painful she recognized for the first time a genuine will to end her life.

Blessed souls are comforted by the aphorism that proclaims when a person hits bottom, they will start to heal. That may be a truism for those who have nails left on their fingers, who have at their disposal tools they can employ to extricate themselves out of a sinkhole. Sadly, however, there might be a corollary to that proposition stating that the vast majority of those visiting the depths of the pit of human anguish lay deadly still while awaiting their demise, for they are without physical, emotional or interpersonal resources to once more do battle with foes as real to them as cartoon characters to a child.

Gyps had cleverly isolated herself from her neighbors while living in the sour belly of New York, and for that matter from associates around the world existing on the streets that had dropped off the slippery side of hope's dreams.

As she gazed around herself that morning, she saw

two of her male colleagues lying not far from her, being sheltered by a stoop. One was motionless under a plastic tarp, his soot-blackened extended hand resting on a cheap bottle of wine. The other was attempting to raise himself up, his arms tenuously holding his upper body upward and his knees bearing the lower body weight—he looked like a dog sniffing a scent.

She sat up and reached into her purse, still stuffed with the money she had dug out of her dirt vault. It was the mirror she sought. Gyps pulled it out and held it close to her face. She stared what seemed to be an endless period of time, contemplating one simple question. Life had become so uncomplicated that it permitted her to delve into the essence of what human existence boiled down to, and it was so elementary it was ridiculous.

"Do I want to continue living?" she asked herself, fogging the mirror with her steamy breath.

She was twenty-nine years old. It wasn't the first time she'd deliberated on her willingness to continue her life. She dried the mirror and replaced it. Then she stood up and gazed around.

Screw it! She proclaimed to the silence of her loneliness. *Screw it!! Screw it!!! Screw it!!!!"* she screeched, her final shrill exhortation ending with a half-hearted shrug.

When she purchased her ticket in New York, the clerk had advised her to buy an open transit, one that would permit her to get off and on as often as she wished so long as she was following her path to Las Vegas.

"You never know, dear, when you'll want to stop for a few days and see a little of the world," the ticket seller kindly advised.

Gyps headed back under a tangle of freeway and train ramps, only a couple blocks to S. Des Plaines Street and back to the Greyhound terminal. She waited four hours before catching the next bus heading west to Vegas. She bought the sandwich she had eyed the day before, and a second one for the road. While sitting at a table alone, she wondered what she might do if by chance the same man who commented on her Juicy Couture was there: she'd never find out.

With her sole possession in the world—other than the purse and small travel bag she carried—a momentary will to live, she was on her way to the city of bright lights.

CHAPTER 9: BACK TO THE UNDERWORLD

There was only one spot in Nevada that might have recognized the heartbeat of this frail and pained soul, and that was the only location she was forbidden to visit, Misty's Place. After everything she had been through, it would have been a logical stopping point to try and connect with mankind.

Gravity had transported her with purpose. Gyps had resolved the big question; she wanted, at least for that moment, to live. Still, she was light years away from being able to embrace the thought of trying to untangle the mess she'd left behind, a world of shame and torment she'd abandoned what seemed a lifetime in the past. Plus, she'd vowed to Misty that she'd never come back.

The terminal was on South Main Street. Holding her travel case in her right hand and grasping her small fortune in her purse with the left, she made the decision to travel south, toward the heart of the city, what visitors and locals refer to as *The Strip*. Gyps knew it well, had been there many times, including enjoying a luxurious suite compliments of Mr. Hugh Crawford, the dear gentleman who, against the admonition of his partner, became the father of her child.

She was also aware of a vast network of underground tunnels beneath some of the most prestigious hotels that Vegas had birthed. On occasion when she'd spend breaks in the city, she'd stop to chat with homeless people. Her charity for the underprivileged and less fortunate stemmed from her own early years when she voluntarily lived the filthy and precarious life of a street person.

Her saving grace during that earlier period of her life was that she never touched, sniffed, smoked, snorted or shot a milligram of any illegal drug, and nearly abstained from alcohol—she discovered that she had one biological blessing in that her chemistry turned the boutique substances most in her position lived for into toxic waste that immediately made her direly ill—she learned that the risk of drug exposure was death for her.

As a result, Gyps represented a rare sample of suffering souls who took their pain straight up, undiluted. Emotional torture had always been a companion. In the caboose of her mind, she had housed a sharp blade and loaded pistol in the event the curses she bore proved to overmatch her willingness to endure. But after what she believed was a resolution she made in Chicago, to keep battling for her existence, she made her way to the rear of the train and cut loose the safely valve she'd always held on to, that "just in case" provision Now she was traveling solo. In the back of her mind, however, was an awareness that she could always pick up replacement tools of self-destruction, if necessary.

As she aimlessly made her way along the streets she noticed a gradual increase in the density of people. Then within a short distance there were crowds, becoming so thick that she recognized a feeling of panic overtaking her. It was a claustrophobic sensation, the knotting of humanity locking her in a sea of flesh from which she began to lose the capacity to breathe, as well as the power of ambulation.

The air was warm and unusually sweltering for a spring afternoon. The frightful sensation of separation from self was unmistakably descending on her. As she experienced the mass of her fellow humans banging and bumping forward into her, and slashing and slamming her from behind, a generalized weakening of her musculature, especially in her legs, came over her.

She glanced to her right side, stretching her neck as if trying to extricate herself from a flood. There, towering above the throng of mankind where she was dissolving to nothingness she saw a giant sign, *MIRAGE*. It may have been the rapid shift of air density—she had just arrived from a Midwest region that had been cursing an obdurate winter-like spring freeze—but the ground beneath her feet began to disappear, followed by bright and successive flashes in her brain, thousands of light bulbs within a fraction of a second randomly dying: she passed out, never experiencing her body as it freefell to the ground.

As the crowd of eager gamblers and joy-seekers stepped over, aside, and at times atop her lame body, she lay unaware. Likely she would have been left for the duration of time it takes for a single soul out of a mob of weekend hedonists to recognize that the creature lying motionless on the ground might actually be a living being. For certain she would have been neglected for a span of time by far exceeding what it took for an unsightly figure that had been peering into the waves of humanity from the upper stairs of Harrah's Hotel to come to her aid.

On the first inspection of his face, his characteristics qualified him as a she rather than he. The strands of his hair were as thin and light as silk, dropping off his head and not resting until reaching well below his shoulders; wisps dangled in front of his face. On the right side of his forehead a tuft turned renegade, shifting direction such that while there was a natural part to the left, this crop of spoilers took off in the opposite direction.

His shabby clothing left no doubt he was not on his way to a job interview. He was wearing a grey t-shirt and baggy nylon warm up pants that no doubt had earned retirement long before he took possession of them. The souls of his shoes had been fastened to the black canvas material with two pieces of thin string on the front and back of each.

But it was the gentleness, narrowness and elongation of the oval shaped face that raised the question of gender. His eyes were soft; there was only a hint of brows but the lashes were long. The nose was narrow and small, and his tiny thin lips pursed, accentuating the chin below as it descended before ending in a distinct point. What punished the tenderness of his face was the skin texture. Deep ravines crossed the forehead from temple to temple like agricultural furrows. The cheeks swelled—resembling Tootsie Rolls—the ends ostensibly serving as braces to hold the nose in place.

Gyps noticed nothing of his appearance as he hoisted her over his shoulder, holding her in place with his right arm and hand while bending over to use his left to grab her purse and travel bag. His strength was manly; his lean but tall body beneath the rags he wore was muscular.

Any members of the crowd sober enough to take notice of his intervention might have wondered if the man coming to her rescue was a relative, except that Gyps' skin was white and pure whereas this man was dark, with a splotchy yellowish brown tone leaving little question that he was an American Indian of one tribe or another.

He carried her for about ten minutes before she resumed consciousness. By then he had managed to reach Paradise Road, a street paralleling Las Vegas Blvd., and a strip of another sort. It was that very short distance off the famous boulevard where life resumed a normalcy, where vagrants could get a quiet night's rest and locals could place a bet for less than a week's earnings; it was also not far from Hampton Hawk's home.

He had laid her next to an east-facing wall of a small building housing a liquor store. The shade, along with Hampton treating her with a wet rag to wipe her brow, permitted Gyps to regain her senses. When she opened her eyes, the she-man was bending over her, positioning her soft case under her head. He didn't say a word, nor did Gyps, who instead unwittingly gaped him.

Realizing she was stable but still weak, he stood up and walked away. The voice she heard coming from within was shrieking at her to get up and run. She knew it was the right thing to do yet at the same time an unconquerable offsetting force outdueled—by only a hair's width—the impulse to flee; worse, it endured long enough that the next recall she had was the odd looking man returning with a plastic bottle of water.

He twisted the cap before handing it to her. Unaware that she was dehydrated, she gulped the entire contents, still without offering a word. In fact, it was Hampton who broke the silence.

"Don't talk," he cautioned in a soft voice. "First you must find your heart. Then you'll be ready for words." He waited several seconds before whispering, though she could barely make out his sentence. "I'll take care of you."

He then sat with his knees pulled toward his chin, his eyes intent on observing Gyps as she deliberated on a most unimaginable circumstance.

Finally he stood and motioned for her to do the same and then to follow him. They walked for close to ten minutes before they came to a wash. There was a wire barrier about three feet high cordoning off the three long concrete channels running parallel, about six feet wide each. There was a break in the fence where it had been severed with wire cutters. Hampton led her through the opening.

They walked about an eighth of a mile before the passageways descended under an overpass used by cars and trucks. Like miners disappearing under the earth, they wandered into the darkness that was periodically illuminated by filtered light coming from above. As they walked, Gyps, a few steps behind the stranger, noticed dwellings not dissimilar to what she had seen under the rail system in New York. She had a peculiar feeling. Was she going back once more to live in the underworld?

Several times she watched as Hampton nodded to

people he knew, though no words were exchanged. After walking about half a mile, making several turns left and right, she was certain she'd not be able to find her way out alone. Still, she had no inclination along the way to turn and flee.

Hampton finally stopped. He took out a flashlight, shining it so that Gyps could see the meager home he had built. Every item was elevated on crates, including a double size bed. He had erected walls on the side to create the impression of a structure, more important to break the wind that at times mercilessly rushed through the tunnels.

He reached under the bed and pulled out a sack. Watching him open the package, she had no idea what it contained, until he began blowing it up. It was an inflatable bed.

"You'll use my bed," he instructed. "You can leave any time you want. I don't advise it until you heal."

For the next two days Hampton cooked meals on his Coleman stove and hovered over her, most of which time she spent sleeping. The emotional turmoil she'd experienced leaving New York and then traveling back to Nevada had battered her already weakened psychological defenses. Hampton recognized the grief she was carrying but never tried to question what the source of her pain might be. Gyps refrained from trying to speak. She also found that as the days passed, that her compulsion to flee any situation coming close to human intimacy ceased in the company of this strange man. She had no wish to take flight.

It was about a week into her guardianship under Hampton's caring hands and eyes—during which time she did not once see the sunlight or blackened night-time sky—when she awakened one morning and let out a shriek. Oddly, she had rested well and had an atypical peaceful sensation initially upon coming to her senses. But once she opened her eyes and gazed about the space she became alarmed to the point of panic.

Hampton had kept a tiny light burning at all times in the event Gyps awakened and was frightened. When she looked about the room on this occasion she noticed the bed where her new friend slept was empty. Her heart raced uncontrollably. But then after exploring the small space within which she was living she realized that the old, smudged and partially torn picture of a woman and little girl he kept on a nightstand along with a small stack of bills weren't missing—she felt a sense of calm knowing he would be returning.

She lay back in the bed. Staring upward at the concrete ceiling, she had no awareness that had she drilled a hole through and then crawled upward she would have ended up in a glitzy ballroom at the Caesar's Palace Hotel. That awareness would have meant little to her, but what did register was that her despair upon awakening was due to her dependence on Hampton.

He had introduced himself simply as Hampton, never

mentioning his surname, Hawk—a perfect description. He seemed to possess the sharp vision of the bird of prey whose name he shared. When he stared at Gyps—which he did often—her impression was that he had the ability to magnify her in his visual field. More important, however, was that he offered to her a quaint sense of comfort and security, unlike any feeling that she'd ever experienced with a man. Never had she been less fearful or more emotionally exposed and vulnerable with a male.

It was typically fairly quiet in the channels where she was now dwelling. But on that morning, she did notice bursts of sound. They were banging noises that were accompanied by reverberations she sensed were coming from the concrete around her. She didn't move. It was less than a half hour before he came back—she was about to see the warrior side of her peaceful protector.

He was running at full speed when he reached his home. Glancing toward the nightstand he grabbed the picture and then the money, shoving both in his pocket.

"Come, quickly," he ordered, still panting. "Leave everything," he shouted.

In his hand was a flashlight. He raced off in the opposite direction from where he approached, Gyps reaching under the bed to pull out the purse with the rest of her life's savings. She then ran, straining to keep up with the man over two decades her senior.

He'd continually glance behind to make sure that she was close to him, twice pausing to grab her arm and entreat her to move faster. She once noticed a rushing sound, eerie and deafening. It reminded her of one of the horror fantasies of Hell she'd had as a child. Something evil was racing toward them, wanting to swallow them live. Hampton heard it too. That's when he'd cock his head to orient to the gushing voice. Then he'd take off in the opposite direction like a crook escaping a finely orchestrated dragnet.

Finally, he made a left turn. They went about a hundred yards. Then Gyps noticed a gradual illumination, as well as the surface of the channel they were jogging on beginning to elevate. They were both moving at a frantic pace. Gyps still had no idea what they were running from, but did have a fleeting thought that Hampton was escaping the law.

That supposition was short lived. Within seconds thunderous roars from the emerging sky above accompanied the swishing noises. God was peeved at something, Gyps wondering if the dodging and racing in the underground was a futile exercise in that He was about to deliver her once and for all to the real Hell she'd been permitted a pass from in New York—had she been undeserving of His leniency?

As they reached the mouth of the channel—a giant orifice from which they were escaping as if it were the stretched-wide-open jaws of a shark—water was pouring down the entrance at a ferocious pace, and with enormous power. Hampton realized at that moment

111

that the deadly force had been moving from both directions to engulf the underworld. He reached back for Gyps' hand. Clasping it firmly, he pulled her against the current as they made their way upward. When they reached the summit, he shoved her to the side to escape the raging water carving a ravine out of the desert floor.

Both lay motionless, exhausted. The sky was unrelenting, torrents of water pounding on their bodies like fire hoses vanquishing an angry mob. The bursts of lightning zigged and zagged across the northern sky, the wild cracks of luminosity creating stick figures that appeared to be tap dancing in a production atop the mountains.

"We're safe now," Hampton assured her. "It's a risk living under. This is the worst I've ever seen."

Gyps glanced at Hampton, the first time permitting a sustained eye contact. Then she started to weep, her tears instantly dissolving into the pool of sandy water she lay in. She cried and cried, never noticing when the storm shrugged, smirked and shoved off to terrorize the group of earth dwellers to the south. Eventually she rolled over on her back, observing Hampton sitting on his buttocks with his legs crossed in front of him. His head was pointed slightly upward and his eyes were shut softly—he appeared in the pose of a guru.

He was beautiful; she was sure for the first time in her life that she could recite the key elements of love.

CHAPTER 10: READY FOR LOVE BUT NOT TRUTH

The storm decimated the homes of about a thousand miners making use of the free real estate under the swanky casinos and restaurants of the Las Vegas Strip. They scrambled out like rats, all leaving behind their priceless belongings, a few unlucky ones drowned. As Gyps was well aware, the town was cold and heartless to those falling on hard times.

What the city excelled at was greeting on a daily basis more sad stories than a mortuary during an entire year. There were scholars that came to Vegas with mathematical equations, dreaming they were the bright ones with a new system sure to break the back of a casino. Beautiful young girls traveled from small cities in Idaho, Texas or Mississippi, believing they could show off their prosperity, a pair of breasts capable of milking a rich industrialist into matrimony…and a life of wealth forever after. Then there were girls whose lone claim to a theatrical career was a high school drama class; they drove into town in old jalopies believing they were there to claim a starring role in the latest sexy Folies Bergere.

Newly graduated black jack dealers or crap table croupiers who had found for the first time in their life that money was rolling in were deluded by a life that was fast, fascinating, furious and fun. Booze flowed, drugs whiffed through the air like lint, and sex was available on demand, for only a couple "C" notes. Better still, they saw the stupidity of the gamblers coming in shift after shift, making one idiotic wager after another and violating every rule of sound betting. They eventually came to believe they had discovered the unique and brilliant idea that they could work the odds in their favor. Then there were the regulars, the ones who routinely brought their paychecks otherwise earmarked for food and rent, believing that luck owed them a hot hand.

Casinos don't go bust owing to wise guys who think they've figured out the final solution to slewing Goliath. Tits and ass get girls laid…and then left. Thrill-seeking kids rolling into town ignorant to the fact that the top theater shows hire actresses with true acting skills, who also happen to be packed with erotic gifts of Mother Nature—or in some cases figures manufactured by Father Plastic Surgeon—call home with tales of fantasy while they're performing "tricks" that would horrify their moms and dads.

The wisest gamblers in the world in dice, cards and wheels stay home. It's the moronic dreamers that end up encountering wives who get sick of eating prayers and promises, and boot their men out long before luck believes them—and if they ever did come home one time a big shot, they blew the winnings in a celebration, returning as quick as they could for a repeat performance only to get the proverbial crap beat out of them, blaming God for forgetting to show up.

Living down below where Gyps was dwelling were samples of lives destroyed by each one of these tragic patterns, and a long list of other plotlines; most get-rich-quick schemers were destined to crash. Yet for some unknown reason, the violent waters had behaved with caprice…there were a few down-under dwellers that came out dry. No such luck for Hampton and Gyps.

The only redeeming factor in the tragedy was that almost as quickly as a torrential rain comes, it leaves. The water level dropped swiftly as it moved on its gravitational journey, leaving in this case a landscape no different than what it had been before. The only change was that belongings might be found two or three miles up channel, if they could ever be recovered.

Hampton, within a few hours, went back under: Gyps shadowed in his wake. There was nothing left. Day after day they scavenged to rebuild a meager space to live—the benefit of their sparse lifestyle was that there was not much to lose and what they'd had was fairly easy to replace. Within a week, they were back in business.

It was an inestimable duration of time that passed—weeks for certain, and a span within which Gyps enjoyed the generosity of her host—before she spoke. She was tidying up after a simple breakfast meal of cooked grains and bananas. The words assumed their own volition and were unmistakably more shocking to her ear than even Hampton's.

"I have money," she expressed, reaching for the purse she now stowed on a small wall cabinet she found in the trash of a nearby home.

Hampton didn't respond. A man of few words himself, he motioned for her to follow; her education in surviving on the streets (under them actually) in Las Vegas was to begin. She'd soon learn that in her new home city, there were opportunities that exceeded even those in New York. In fact, during the course of the next few months, Gyps would become a skilled practitioner at taking advantage of other people's carelessness and inebriation.

A gambler at a blackjack table might be making bets of thousands of dollars per hand. An attractive woman cheering next to him could do magic, exciting him to believe the strange lady is his lucky charm, earning hundred dollar chips as gifts for bringing good fortune. The slot machines were also a fine source of revenue. It was common knowledge that people playing what used to be called the one-arm bandits were the most foolish of any gamblers. To prove the point, not infrequently after being discouraged by one too many losing spins, a player might walk away from the machine that had been entrancing them for hours, only to forget that their ticket still had money on it.

Finally, there was the floor.

"Always walk with your head down," Hampton lectured. "People gambling are often drunk. They carry around stacks of chips. After leaving a table they may carelessly stuff them in their pockets or with equal mindlessness reach to take out a handful. A chip might then roll unnoticed. I've found thousands of dollars assuming the sad pose."

While Gyps was increasing her wealth under Hampton's tutelage, she noticed he never asked her for a penny. Finally one afternoon by chance she observed him walking into a store with post office boxes. She stopped outside and watched as he used his key to open a box. There was a sole envelope and he took out what she was sure was a check. He endorsed it and then went up to the clerk. He was given an envelope that he addressed, handing it back to the man before turning to leave.

When he reached the door, there was Gyps, staring as if she had witnessed him naked, which she never had. He walked to the rear of the building where a small bench had been placed under an awning for anyone caring to have a snack in the shade.

"You've never told me your name."

"It's Rose; my name is Rose," Gyps lied.

"Rose, I don't need money. You've seen the picture I keep," he mentioned, referring to the frayed color print of a plump dark-skinned woman and a lean young girl—both with a skin tone similar to Hampton's. "That's my wife and daughter; my girl is named Ekta, which in my language, Apache, means *Unity*."

Hampton spoke her name with sorrow that was notable in his eyes. Gyps watched him as he was speaking, saddened to see him in such grief.

"Before she was born, I had an affair. I didn't know my wife was pregnant. But after finding me out, she did the right thing. She packed a suitcase and when I came home that night from what I believed was a secret affair, it was sitting on the stoop of our home. For my people, the act was symbolic. I had been put out."

"But couldn't you apologize or do something to try and mend it?" Gyps asked, not recognizing that she was engaging in her first sustained conversation in almost twelve years.

"Once the twig of a woman's heart is broken, it can never be repaired. Don't ever forget that. Some day you will find love."

"I have. I love you," she expressed, startled by the conviction in her words.

"Our hearts beat the same rhythm of pounding pain, it's like two beings sharing a single footprint. I could see and feel that when I first saw you; that's why I came after you. I pray that someday your soul will mend."

Gyps peered at the man with whom she knew she shared a deep connection. It was not a carnal love, she was certain of that. It was the feeling of safety, being accepted without condition, the quietness of her mind in his presence, the tenderness and giving with no expectation of return on his part, the knowing that no matter what she did she would never be able to terminate the bond they shared.

Then why did she lie about her name, and later about every detail of her background? Hampton, as he sat across from her, gazing at her face while she delivered words he recognized as untruth, understood that insecurity was serving as master, yet she was impotent to fight back.

Perhaps that was why he never pushed her to speak, knowing that for some people at distinct intersections of their lives, each syllable was a building block in a fiction necessitated when reality, with all its assumed candor and probity, would be far more damaging and destructive.

"Have you mended from your suffering?"

"No. It's too late for me in The Shadow World," Hampton expressed sadly, referring to how his people described our own here-and-now world. "My girl has gone to The Real World, a place of potential, power and truth."

"What happened?" Gyps asked, finding an urgency to know more about her soul partner.

"You want my story?" he chuckled. "I've never told it," he added sheepishly. "I can't tell you why I kept it to myself all those years before she died, but afterward everything changed and I, like you, quit communicating entirely with my fellow man."

"How do you know I haven't been talking?"

"Because your soul-chatter is screeching."

"You can hear it?"

"Anyone can who cares to listen will hear it," Hampton smiled. "Most people are too busy to pay attention."

"I don't want anyone to pay attention to me," she moaned.

"You must remain silent until you realize how desperate you are to be heard." Hampton touched her cheek softly, his eyes softening to invite her to visit. "Now you can listen to my tale. Since you came into my life, for the first time in five years I've wished for someone to pay attention to me. I've been waiting for you, Rose.

"I was only nineteen when I married. Immediately my wife must have become with child. So after she banished me from her life, it was logical to her that I would not be permitted a role in the rearing of my daughter. I abided by her wish and to be honest, other than the single picture you've seen that was sent to me by my brother, I've never seen nor talked to my little girl.

"I never remarried. I did go to school and became a cook; eventually I became a master chef here in Vegas. Call me a martyr but I devoted my life to supporting them. Almost every cent I made I mailed faithfully to my wife. As my career went on, obviously, there was more and more to enrich their lives. Then five years ago, I received a note from my wife telling me my daughter had been killed, hit by a drunk driver on the reservation. Cruelly, she blamed me, using the occasion to inform me that the child had been doomed at birth owing to my dishonor.

"I didn't go back to work. I walked out of my apartment and never returned, leaving behind my minimal possessions. I later discovered that I had a substantial pension and retirement benefits that were to be sent to me monthly. I found out that my daughter had married and had two young ones, my grandchildren. So each month I do what you saw today, I mail them the check."

"But if you have money to live, why come to the channels and why scrimp off the tricks you've taught me?"

"Punishment. It's all been to inflict pain on myself. But gradually I think I'm finding peace. I taught myself to meditate. My studies have advanced. Someday I'll teach you what I've learned."

Faithful to his word, twice a day he and Gyps would spend an indeterminate amount of time in silent prayer.

Their life together went on for another six years. Then one day two simultaneous and related events occurred.

After the morning session of mediation Hampton made an announcement, the first of the curiously related two matters.

"Gyps, I've been deliberating for some time now. I love being a chef; it was my way of expressing my inner self, an outlet for my creative side. I'm going to make inquiries."

"I'll go with you," she offered.

"No. You're not being called yet."

Gyps' initial reaction was to weep. Oddly, she felt fright at being alone again. Still, she offered no further resistance.

"I had no choice, Rose. My tragedy was imposed. For you that's not the case."

"But I can't..."

"You can drown as quickly in shallow water as an ocean. First you must learn to swim. Be patient," he advised.

Gyps still had not disclosed the source of her shame but surmised that Hampton knew it was self-inflicted.

Later that morning, Hampton went out. Shortly after he left, Gyps did the same. As she was wandering the streets she decided to sit on a park bench. Somebody had left a newspaper. It had been read thoroughly, opened to the sixth page. Glancing at it Gyps noticed on the bottom right corner a short article, the title sending a shiver through her spine. It was titled, *"Upscale Brothel's Chef to Retire."*

She grabbed the paper and held it close to her face, reading every word several times.

> *"Misty's Place, the ritzy brothel almost an hour outside of Las Vegas, will soon be looking for a new chef. Bernard Pepin, the world recognized gastronomic master, has been treating their esteemed clientele for the past twenty-two years of his illustrious career. At seventy-seven years of age he said his knees had worn out and he might be needing replacement surgeries."*

Gyps tore out the piece and folded it. She put it in her pocket. Later that afternoon, she took it out.

"Look at this," she said to Hampton. "You wanted a job. It might be perfect. You wouldn't have to work as intensely as some restaurants might demand and you'd still be able to use your imagination as you please."

Of course, Gyps knew the requirements of the position. She was well acquainted with the famous Chef Pepin, often talking with him while he was in the kitchen. Owing to his orthopedic condition already deteriorating due to decades of being on his feet for his work, the lighter demands at Misty's made it a perfect position for Pepin; ideal for Gyps' mentor and father figure to be his successor.

When she brought it to his attention she knew if he did apply, and then was accepted, it would be unsettling to her life. She shuddered at the thought she might have to move on again to prevent the chance of being drawn back into her old life, especially having to face Misty and then possibly her child, wherever he or she might be.

Gyps had recently passed her thirty-fifth birthday. Misty was two years short of reaching the half century milestone. Two years before, Star had passed on applying for a driver's license, vowing she'd revisit the matter in the future. Hampton was the precise age that Chef Pepin was when the master had begun his role as chief of food preparation at Misty's, fifty-five.

Hampton would secure the job at Misty's Ranch, though the famed establishment had changed measurably and unimaginably since Gyps had left.

CHAPTER 11: THE INTERVIEW

It's the same old story, we investigate and research, explore options and choose what we believe is the best plan for our life under a given condition or circumstance. But in the end, life proves to be nothing but a massive casino where we find our destiny rolled out like a pair of dice in a game of craps, pulled from a deck of cards at a blackjack table, swung from a wheel of fortune, or spun like a symbol on a disc to land randomly into small spaces on the face of a slot machine.

What it means is that in spite of our diligence and determination, events—especially ones we consider negative—unfold in ways they convince us that we had no control over them. For some the mishaps of life are worse than for others, for some bad luck comes more frequently, for some misadventures arrive in bundles, and then there are those who are delivered hardship quick and nasty.

Gyps had no way of knowing but during the last year of her rooming with Hampton, Misty suffered a tragic and sudden loss. It took all of a few seconds for the madam to be disabled, an equally short span of time for the face of Misty's Ranch to change forever, and for the life of young Star to be momentously impacted.

It was near midnight on a routine evening. Misty began to experience another of the familiar headaches. This time, however, for the first time, rather than abating after a few seconds, as had been the case on every prior occasion, the pain was followed immediately by a sensation of electrical shock shooting through her brain. As she reached to grab her head, she keeled over and then fell on the floor. She passed out. Had it not been for the fortuitous coincidence of a retired neurosurgeon being a guest when the mishap occurred, her post-stroke recovery might have been worse; or she may not have survived the neurological accident.

Here was a lady with none of the risk factors that might have predicted her a likely candidate for a medical emergency of this type—except perhaps one might fault her for not heeding the early warning signs. Still, she ate well and generally was in excellent health. She abstained from tobacco, alcohol and drugs. She typically rested, and she exercised moderately—she was dealt a full house but Mercury was in retrograde; a lousy straight flush put a savage beating on her.

The cerebrovascular event causing an abrupt loss of blood supply to the cerebellum was disastrous, but not fatal. Misty would be rushed to the hospital where she would spend two months between emergency treatment and then rehabilitation. When she returned home, she had her work cut out for her. Sadly, for all practical purposes she was retired from her role as madam—her main function in that regard was to advise her replacement.

That's right, in the waiting was the one person who could handle the assignment, Star. She had grown up; oh had she. Even before Misty's downfall, Star had matured into a remarkable young lady, a fact evident to anyone having contact with her.

In the main hall most evenings after Misty's crisis, the remarkable and stunning Star could be found doing what she had unwittingly done as a child, mimicking the gestures and acts of her acting mom. As if from a similar genetic sample, she shared with Misty many characteristics over and above elegance, beauty and charm. She was every bit as bright and when it came to business, she was dogged. There had been no loss of income after Misty's mishap. Instead, profits had climbed an impressive six percent despite a horrid economic climate. The clientele embraced and respected her. It was almost as if she was Misty.

One afternoon there was quite a bit of excitement in the main hall. Star could be seen talking it up with a couple of men near the bar. It would have been difficult to discern from a distance if she was speaking Russian or another similar language. Two of the girls, Allie and Brie, were being introduced to the men.

Then Star noticed Daisy, another of her crew, was welcoming a woman coming in through the front door. What struck Star was the incongruousness of this lady's appearance. Star chuckled as she thought either the woman was colorblind or playing a Bohemian character out of a Renoir painting. Reds with oranges, green shades with fleshy-pink tones, blues with bright yellows; her dress was a celebration of light and contrast.

Star also observed what she thought were quirky movements of her body as Daisy led the visitor to a sofa to have a seat. After settling the guest, Daisy walked over to Star and whispered in her ear. Star nodded and left the men in the company of their dates. She then went to greet the eccentric woman.

As she approached, the lady stood. She moved toward Star and reached out first to grab her, and then fully enveloped her in a bear hug. After she released her subject, she freely shook her whole body as if her introductory words couldn't be discharged before first releasing her physical enthusiasm.

"Hi, I'm Deze," she pronounced with a long "e" at the end, gracefully displaying her French accent. "In

English you have the word 'dizzy,'" she giggled. "Some people think I am, but no," she sung out with a cheery rise in tone, "I'm Deze. It's so good...to meet you, Star... Star, Star, oh, I could say it all day," she gushed, her pitch elevated.

The zany woman was prone to speech with tonal patterns fluctuating wildly, at times sounds ejaculating in rapid bursts.

"Thanks for coming," Star calmly responded to Deze's animation.

"This I would not miss. *What is this young madam like?* In my head, over and over, I wondered. Star," Deze remarked, pausing to again wrap her in a hug, after which she stepped back to admire the living creature, "I couldn't wait."

"Well, here I am," Star retorted, oddly flattered. "Come sit down and we'll talk."

Star led Deze to a table where they could sit across from one another. Deze examined the space. Then she lifted the chair and placed it snugly close to Star.

"My boss, he says to me," Deze mimicking a huffy sound, "people buy magazines to hear about famous people or unusual stories. I don't see this one for our readers. Quel dommage," she squealed. "I let him talk. So how did Deze get him to see the light?"

"I don't know," Star tittered.

"You ask? I'll tell you. Mr. Big Shot, big, big hot...he thinks because he's the editor of Play Time Magazine he owns the world. Star, he's worse than a dictator; uh, where was I...yes, when he heard about this beautiful young lady, the famous madam, who was born in a brothel and had never left her whole life, he stood up right then, proclaiming like The Emperor he believes he is, as if it was his idea, 'This is a story that has to be told.'"

"I'll tell you whatever you want to know," Star offered.

"Everything. Every silly unimportant little detail; each tiny snowflake of a winter storm..." she spun out her words as she spontaneously rose and swirled herself several revolutions before ending up facing a wall with several pictures. "I want to know everything."

On the table was a small platter with finger sandwiches. Deze took one and popped it in her mouth, her eyes widening as she chewed and then swallowed.

"Who is the master of this French treat?" Deze swooned.

"We have a new chef. There he is over there," Star said, pointing to Hampton who in his white uniform was conversing with the bartender.

Deze, her senses overwhelmed, permitted herself to race over to the man. Her words couldn't be heard by Star but the visible expressions of her face and movement of her arms, followed by a volunteer hug, made it certain she was praising the man. After paying deserved respect, she went back to Star.

"The greatest restaurants of the world would want a man who could create a taste that makes the whole body tickle. You are a smart one to keep this trophy," Deze glistened.

She was standing, noticing one of the pictures on the wall. She pointed at it jubilantly. "That's yours!" she finally declared.

"Right. It's a piece I did of one of my girls, Toni," Star revealed.

"Magnificent. O, la, la. You have the strokes of Cezanne, such vision and charm." She moved to the next piece hanging next to the Cezanne. "And this?" she questioned, as she began reading the text. "Handsome. You did this too?"

Star answered by nodding affirmatively.

"It is bold, firm," she announced, thrusting her hands to the sides of her head in a gesture of utter shock. "The mind of a man in a women's spirit. And this one?" she wondered out loud, staring at the following item on the wall.

"That's Misty's Ranch when it opened; it's grown quite a bit over the years. You see Misty is a bright lady. She envisioned a brothel that offered, believe it or not, much more than straight sex. She dreamed of something more like...a resort; an entity where men could eat, socialize, relax and of course—"

"I know. I know!" Deze interrupted. "So this place, it's like smearing mustard and loading up relish on a hot dog at a baseball game...so delicious, they can't resist in the end; oh, la, la...la, la." She paused as if she were about to deliver a clandestine battle plan to an eagerly awaiting group of officers. She spoke in a hush. "Okay, are you ready? Now Deze tells you a secret. Every girl has a fantasy, right? For American girls, what is it?"

"I'm not sure," Star responded.

"It's Cinderella," she cheered, as she bestowed her grand insight on Star. "It's to be rescued from sadness by the fair prince. But in France, it's different. We are more...dangerous, risqué. And me," she chuckled. "God save my soul, my dream..." she savored the moment of disclosure by reaching out to take Star's hand and then, with an imploring expression, she gently touched the side of her face, "Oh, I hope you will not think unfavorably of me, but I would want to be a prostitute." With the disclosure, she surrendered to a reverie.

"To lay myself down for every lonely, heart-broken, desperate and impassioned man...to serve the beast." She then continued with a note of farcical hostility. "To give him something for the rest of his life he'll be searching to repeat but never find...to know I did it without a care in the world." Again she took a break, this time spicing the story with a splash of mockery. "Will he call me back, will he tease my heart or will he love me?" she dramatically posed. "Oh, to not care, to never be abandoned and left in anguish...not one more pitiful time...and then to be paid!!" she smirked as she stared beseechingly into Star's face. Finally she whispered to her. "And your fantasy, mon cher? The whole world is waiting to hear."

Star's brief response was delivered with a girlish laughter. "I don't have a fantasy."

"Oh, but you must. It's too sad to live without dreams. Deze will find out what yours is before she leaves. Yes, she will."

"Okay," Star replied with bewilderment.

"All your life, right here at Misty's?" she mused. "You've never left; even once? Tres extraordinaire."

"People think so, but—"

"Star, have you ever wanted to go?"

"I've thought about it. But then I forget about leaving. I'll admit that sometimes I wonder if it's fear."

"No, no, my dear; it's destiny. Love will determine your fate," Deze decreed.

"I'm loved here. My life has been blessed with love."

"So bright. So beautiful! So full of life." She deliberated before revealing a great discovery. "That's why they call you Star...don't forget, Deze told you."

"No, I won't."

How will I ever write everything about this Star, raised her entire life in a brothel? Deze mused openly while holding a pencil.

"There's a lot I have to tell you," Star offered.

"Oh, and you will, you will."

"You may not understand that it's not only that I had people who loved me, I had—"

"My Star. My Star. A child needs...culture," she drew out the word, "and what the French call liberte. How can you get that in a brothel?"

"I didn't know where I was raised until I was almost twelve. And after that, most of what went on here, Misty separated me from; my life was a strict program of learning, enrichment...and culture. I had no exposure to drugs or alcohol. I had a more refined life than almost any child who was raised outside.

"Such imagination," Deze commented, unwittingly humoring Star.

"It's true. My life has been proper and clean, quite far from obscene. It's been tasteful if not pure, I assure.

As Star spoke the last sentence her voice became sonorous, owing to her overhearing the sound of a tune coming from an adjacent room where several of her girls were in the middle of a waltz lesson under the direction of their dance maestro, Mr. Molliere.

By now the main room was empty, so Star swung open the large doors adjoining the two spaces. She had an idea she thought might help to convey the point she was trying to make to Deze.

"Please, wait a moment," Star called out to Deze.

Star then went up to Mr. Molliere. "Could you bring the girls in here for a minute, please?"

Mr. Molliere led the group of ladies into the hall where Deze was interviewing Star.

"Girls, show this lady what you've been working on in dance this week," Star requested.

The music began and Mr. Molliere led the girls in a short waltz routine. All the while Star was humming lines she thought might not only fit with the music but also dispel any misconceptions that Deze might have about her upbringing:

"I can waltz with a flair, I've been showered for hours with care, by design it's no shrine but I promise my home, it's honestly fine." She glanced at Deze to be sure she still had her attention. "And like most, I've been handed a few reprimands for slippin' that diction of mine." Then she winked at the wistful woman. "I can stun, old and young, when I define a wine with the touch of my tongue, but go search and you'll see it's no church I agree, though I promise it's plenty pristine for me."

Star pointed to Mr. Molliere teaching the girls. "We're running a high-end resort. Sure, there's bits of dirt but we mask them well. You'll find sin, you'll find whores being whores, but you'll find it behind closed doors. And you can quote me you won't see The Pope comin' close, but I promise my home is as decent as most."

"But, Star. This is—"

Star put her finger to her mouth, gesturing to Deze that she wasn't finished speaking about her life. "I can speak with a grace that would ease you to a peaceful place, but it's doubtless you won't see no countess or earl, but I promise my house has been fit for a girl."

As she finished edifying Deze about her privileged life, the ensemble of girls was waltzing. Then Mr. Molliere presented himself with a bow to Deze, taking her hand to invite her to join in a dance—her excitement oozed.

"The waltz is the Mont Blanc of dance, the highest peak of romance," Deze panted to Star as she returned after partnering with the maestro.

"I could see that watching you," Star complimented the lady who was delirious with joy."

"You've had no romance yet; none at all?"

"Not really," Star admitted.

"But you had to have a boyfriend."

"No, never," she revealed. "Well, there was a boy I used to think about when I was younger, but he was too old, I was too young and... he went away. From then on, from what I've seen, men aren't for me."

"I told you; didn't Deze tell you?"

"What?" Star giggled.

"That Deze would find your fantasy," she teased. "Too old, too young; too fat, too skinny; too rich, too poor; too smart, too dumb. Who cares? Find that boy! He'll open your heart and you'll find answers to all the questions that confuse you."

"I don't know," Star pondered.

"Well, you think about it. But Deze is always right."

Deze stood. She started gathering papers that she

had placed in front of her, ones she had never looked at. Haphazardly she stuffed them into her satchel.

"What will I say? What will I say about my Star, my little madam, so full of love but without a lover?"

"Are you leaving...already?" Star asked, perplexed by the quick exit when she'd been told that Deze wanted a lengthy interview for an article.

"Deze's done."

"But I hardly told you—"

"I know everything," Deze promised. "You'll see, every miniscule grain of sand stores an entire history; Star, Star, wait and see—"

"Will I get a copy of what you write?"

"Deze will bring it herself...and if I need a job..."she reached to embrace Star again, this time receiving a fine hug in return, "I hope you'll be hiring," she laughed.

"Being a prostitute isn't for everyone...I think you may be better off keeping it a fantasy," Star advised.

"Then thank you," Deze whispered, "and we'll keep it our little secret."

"Can you wait a minute?" Star inquired.

"But of course."

Star was gone only a few minutes before returning. In her hand was a photo, about three inches by five. She showed it to Deze.

"That's my mother. I've never shared this with anyone," Star admitted. "She died when I was born. When I was growing up Crystal was one of the girls that I was very close to. She knew my mom well. She retired and left a few years ago. Then right after that, I received a letter from her with the picture enclosed. She asked me not to let Misty know I had it; she thought that Misty would be angry with her if she knew she'd given it to me. So I've kept it to myself."

Deze for the first time since she arrived was solemn, her demeanor presenting an unprecedented state of quietude.

"I was thinking of talking to some of the girls before writing my piece. Could I reach this Crystal?"

"Of course, but why?" Star questioned.

"I don't know. Just that it sounds like an interesting angle to the story."

"I'll have the contact information for Crystal and a couple others who helped raise me emailed to you later today, if that'll be okay."

"Perfect," Deze responded. Then she took out her cell phone. "I'd love to snap a picture of your mother if you don't mind."

Star, caught off guard by the odd request said nothing. Deze took two shots.

"How did you like it…your interview?" Deze posed, her normal dramatics creeping back into her outward presentation.

"It was everything I didn't expect."

"Deze is usually everything Deze didn't expect," she clowned.

Star walked Deze to the door to leave, the guest one last time securing her in a warm embrace.

"No mother. No romance," Deze muttered, shaking her head in disbelief. "You'll see. Love will come to you."

CHAPTER 12: RIVALRY AND STRATEGIC BETRAYAL

It was a slow, gradual process of healing. Misty was encouraged not only by the progress she'd made toward her recovery but also by the prognosis of the neurologist and rehabilitation counselors. She was assured that after a cerebral event such as she experienced, improvement was expected to be measurable during the following two-year period. Then, after that she could expect only minor improvement. Nevertheless, her prospects were heightened due to the resources at her disposal, a fact she embraced appreciably—she had knowledgeable professionals, a critical factor toward helping to craft a program that would maximize gains.

Every day she would do a range of exercises to facilitate recovery of her balance, and orientation of movement in space. While she was faithful and disciplined in her efforts, she had to battle through the muckiness and cloudiness of her emotions; she was depressed. It was not uncommon for her to fly off in a rant when her compromised tolerance for failure was exceeded; whoever might be around—sadly Star the most likely—she'd treat with savage ridicule, worsening her mood when after the outburst she'd suffer the humiliation of a teary apology.

When she'd stare in the mirror, it would enrage her. She was as elegant in appearance as she had ever been, as long as she stood still or sat. Upon ambulation the entire picture went out of focus. That's when she'd have to face the reality that she was only a portion of the person she'd once been. Most discouraging for her was the realization that she'd never make a full recovery, and never again be able to play head coach to her crew of pro love makers.

That's not to say she wasn't proud of Star. She was. In fact, while it was no surprise to her that Star could rise to the occasion and step in as madam, she admired the remarkable devotion her adopted daughter showed toward her role. As far as she was concerned, Star would be the perfect person to keep Misty's Ranch on a growth trajectory.

As is the case in all situations where there is more than one person with a vested interest, there would surely be differences of opinion—this child did have a father, a mighty powerful one at that. Misty had been set back, was weakened, but had every bit of her wits about her. Even in her compromised condition, she would never stand back from a quarrel.

Sitting in her office trying to concentrate on some of the administrative functions she was handling to assist Star, Misty received a surprise guest—Hugh Crawford. He was one of the few outsiders she'd permitted to see her. Actually Hugh had been supportive of her infirmity to the extent he had experts flown in to evaluate Misty, and took a hand in orchestrating the post-hospital treatment program.

"So, how is business?" Hugh beamed.

"You mean how amazingly well is your daughter doing?"

"She's a jewel, isn't she," he burst out with laughter. "Not even twenty years old and she's already mastered her trade. I'm so impressed, I think it may even be time she takes this world by storm."

"She's happy," Misty responded curtly, sensing what was coming.

"Right. But she doesn't know any different. Maybe she's capable of more. What do you think about giving her the opportunity to find out?"

"You tell me who could have more opportunity," Misty sneered. "She speaks six languages fluently, she had the educational equivalent of several masters' degrees, she's cultured in the arts and sciences and…she's got her hands full right here…and isn't going anywhere."

"Misty, for god sakes wake up. She's my daughter and I've been reasonable up to this point. But I think it's time for her to see something other than the inside of a whorehouse."

"What the hell do you call your precious hotels?" she contentiously fired at him.

"I'm talking about the best universities, travel, associates and friends...what about marriage and family?" he posed calmly to her. "Did it ever cross your mind that these things are normal? Let her decide if she wants them...it's time," he decreed.

"I knew this all along; you've given me plenty of hints, haven't you? You never planned to keep our deal," she snapped. "So what is it? You want to come riding into Star's life on your white stallion and whisk her off to a land of fluffy pink clouds."

"She's at an age where it may be now or never," he barked, trying to control his fury so as to most effectively deliver his next point. "I want my daughter back!"

"You never had your daughter," Misty shouted. "You chose to give her up. That was the arrangement we both agreed to. You don't remember that?" Misty stood to face him straight on, her rage contributing to her needing to secure herself by holding the edge of the table. "Don't make me play my hand. This is the last thing your wife wants to know about."

Hugh glared at her. Misty never flinched. She did attempt to back him off, unconsciously resorting to using guilt and shame tokens that she was holding in her mental bank account.

"You waited until I was down. You call yourself a man?"

Hugh would have no part of it. He turned to leave, then halted to address another possible consideration.

"If it's about money, the effect it will have on the business...you know I'll cover everything."

Misty looked at him as if he were a loon. He knew as well as her that she was wealthy in her own right. Still, Hugh had no inclination to defend himself. His mind had shifted toward hatching an alternative plan.

Hugh Crawford was the type of male who never left success to chance. He was a bright and well-educated man who knew the formula for attaining wealth included hard work, perseverance, resilience, dedication and pugnacity. He also recognized that in some instances cleverness, cunning and even a sprinkle of deceit were unavoidable elements for executing a favorable strategy.

"It was all part of the game," he'd argue if speaking to an imaginary moralist—even to his own superego—one that unfairly refused to pardon his misbehaviors. "If I act with complete candor, I'll get slaughtered. Don't get me wrong. I'd never lie to a business partner or associate. But I'm aware that conditions and circumstances change and the terms agreed upon at one point in time might not be manageable at a later date. Creativity, flexibility and imagination! You can't survive in my world without them."

Misty wouldn't dare claim ignorance. She anticipated from the start what was going to happen; she simply didn't know when or how the betrayal would take place—she was about to find out.

Hugh left Misty at The Ranch and went immediately back to his office. He was seething. The short trip driving in the car was dedicated toward deliberating options. Before he arrived at his building, he came upon what he thought was the perfect plan to force little Star out of the cell Misty had locked her in.

There was nothing that happened in the state of Nevada that Hugh Crawford didn't know about. He was aware that his son had, on a couple occasions, visited Misty's Ranch with his buddies. He'd taken a similar excursion during his early years and perceived tutoring from a skilled prostitute to be a vital educational experience. What he did not know was that his son had no interest in the girls' professional expertise but had been enraptured with Star—the fact that she was his half-sister an unknown to the son but, of course, not to Hugh or Misty.

The man should have had the good sense to leave snoozing puppies doze, let Star sort out her destiny without his direct influence. But he had suppressed a powerful paternal instinct for far too long, and that coupled with his giant sized ego was about to give the man an unexpected twist to the tale.

When he reached his office, he sat pensively for a few moments, dazing at a pile of documents his secretary had placed on his desk for his signature. Finally, he picked up his phone and pressed a single button.

"This is Hugh Crawford," he announced authoritatively. "If the Governor is in would you ask him if he has a moment?"

There was a brief silence, Hugh grinning as he contemplated outfoxing Misty.

"Ah, Harold, how are you?" He paused to listen to the Governor groan about his problems. "Who is it you're sending over?" Again he waited to hear his friend pose a question to him. "Of course. I know them both quite well." The Governor quickly embellished on his worrisome state. "You don't lose a wink of sleep over this, partner," Hugh boasted. "I backed you into office and I'll be damned if I'll let anyone push you out." His tone turned to contempt. "By hook or crook, one way or another, I'll take care of this bastard. I'll be in touch."

Pure dumb luck; you get a taste of it occasionally, he chuckled to himself as he hung up.

An hour later, his buzzer went off.

"Good, good, good," he chirped pleasantly to his secretary. "Send them right in."

There were two men that had been ordered by the Governor to present themselves at Hugh's office. The

146

secretary ushered them in. Leading was Obbie, a small man. He had short thick brown hair with a heavy application of grooming gel. This thick substance allowed the owner to part it meticulously on the left side and then comb it such that it beckoned to be mussed by a naughty lady in the mood for a devilish tease. What would make such a gesture all the more alluring was his babyish face, upon which he sported a pair of wire-framed glasses.

Following Obbie, who definitely looked the part of the consummate intellectual, was a fellow making up for any inches subtracted from his partner. His name was Walt. He was elongated with height exceeding Hugh by an obvious measure. Then, rather than the rigid gait exhibited by Obbie, he ambled with a looseness that made his legs appear to be dancing while his upper body labored to maintain an erect posture.

"Sit. Sit. Sit, gentlemen. So tell me, what have I been missing out on at the Governor's Mansion?"

"Like always, he's dreaming and scheming for Washington," Obbie responded in his characteristic anxious manner. His voice squeaked, an infuriating feature one had to be tolerant not to offend.

"We just may get him there before this is over. Imagine," Hugh said dreamily, "our own Nevada governor going to the White House."

"Not with the direction things are headed in now," Obbie responded despairingly. "He's being cooked... cooked."

"Is it that bad?"

"Here, look at this," Obbie advised, thrusting a newspaper across the desktop for Hugh's perusal. "And this, and this, and this..."he winced as he took one document after another from his briefcase and handed them to Hugh. "We're behind in every poll; we're losing...losing... losing," he declared with an irritating histrionic snivel.

Hugh rose imperiously. "Do you know who his chief strategist was when he was elected?"

"No," Obbie answered meekly.

"Me," Hugh roared. "And I'll do the same to make sure he's re-elected. You bet your hard-on, I will."

"It's my fault, my fault," Obbie whined. He dramatized his next statement by grabbing his neck with both hands and squeezing upward, forcing his words to be gagged. "I feel like killing myself."

On the walls were various pieces of art and western-style objects. Hugh was a big fan of rodeo riding and in the corner of the office was a replica of a bronco in the convoluted form of bucking. Draped over the head was a lasso. Walt picked it up and just as Obbie was releasing his neck, he tossed him the rope. Obbie, irked by the dismissive act, stomped his foot.

"Sir," Walt took over, "the governor's key opponent, Lonnie Lilly—"

"My Lord! A name like, Lonnie Lilly," Hugh spit. "We're going to elect a man for Governor with a name that sounds like a goddamn pussy cat. Huh. Over my dead body," he shouted but rather than pounding his desk he tapped it confidently.

"If I may, Mr. Crawford, let me explain that Lilly is branding my boss as the state leader in sin and smut. He's giving him a shameful upbraiding."

"We're losing," Obbie whimpered, leaning back in his chair as if defeated.

"Obbie, I thought you hung yourself," Walt playfully teased a partner whose antics he excused owing to his awareness that in spite of Obbie's tenuous emotional balance, he was a brilliant thinker. "Anyway, it's this new element, the clean, mainstream industry; that's what's hurting us. You see, they're all about basic family values...morals are their mantra. They talk religion, the word of their god; well, god better help us because we're getting slaughtered."

"You know the old saying, god helps those who help themselves. Well, we'll help ourselves all right. We're going to beat that double-dealing rascal at his own game."

"Lilly and his people think they can take the state in a whole different direction," Walt continued. "And that duplicitous schmuck is preaching to these puritan hogs who if they had it their way would turn Nevada into... Idaho...morbid thought."

"It's my fault. I should have seen it," Obbie sighed.

"This Lilly, Pansy...hell, whatever flower he is, he wants duplicity, does he? Well, I'll give him duplicity...

and throw in a bathtub of good old-fashioned dishonor," Hugh proclaimed triumphantly.

"No question about it. Whatever we we're called on to do, we'll do it," Walt pronounced like an obedient soldier.

"Let me think," Hugh deliberated as he sat down.

Obbie jumped up. He looked like a geeky demon.

"Prostitution! Get rid of the whores who shame our fine state!" he decreed roguishly. "Shut them down!!"

His outburst deepened the state of contemplation Hugh was engaged in. Walt stared nonplussed at his wacko partner before countering the perceived idiocy of his outcry.

"That's ingenious. Let's see...every hotel in the state cleans up their prostitution; so revenue from hotel rooms, gambling and entertainment...and of course prostitution itself plummets. Obbie, why don't you just write the concession speech now? Do you realize what you're proposing, betraying the base of support we have?" Walt ridiculed.

"Wait. He has a point," Hugh commented deliberatively.

"With all respect, sir, my pea size brain can't see anything but disaster."

"Walt, nobody pays attention when the showgirls, cocktail waitresses and change girls at our hotels occasionally take a trick on the side; it's not really visible.

But these virtue seekers...purists, they sure as hell take interest in whorehouses."

"They're the grime of the grime; the filth of the state!" Obbie chimed in. "Shut them down!" he reiterated his prior mandate.

"We don't need to shut them all down," Hugh explained deliriously. "Just one. Just one will do it, boys. Our Governor will take a spear to this sweet lily pod. Then once he lances him a good one, he'll roast the duplicitous schmuck on a spit. Our Governor is to become the champion of a new branding campaign," Hugh announced as if introducing a boxer. "Meet the Governor of...The New Nevada."

"Just one?" Obbie peeped out.

"Yes," Hugh smiled delightedly as he embraced his epiphany. "We close down Misty's Ranch and—"

"But you personally protect her place," Obbie protested.

"Obbie, don't worry about it," Hugh emphasized with a hand gesture delivered to silence the opposition.

"But closing down only one won't do any—"

"Don't—"Hugh heightened his hand movement as a warning.

"But it's not fair to—"

"Worry—"

"But—"Obbie still objected.

"About it!" Hugh completed his admonishment as if

talking to a child. "Now, Obbie, it's your idea...and it's divine."

"How do we do it?" Walt voiced to introduce the practical side of the operation.

"WE do not do it...Obbie does," Hugh chuckled.

"Let me rid the state of every one of those smut buckets. I want them all smashed to pieces," he devoutly shouted, his own moral mission interfering with him taking instruction from Hugh.

"Obbie, you'll do just what I'm asking of you, understood?" Hugh ordered. "You'll go to Misty's...and you'll get all the proof we need to justify a slug of code violations—"

"What codes?" Walt laughed. "Prostitution is perfectly legal in that county."

"Walt, you're a great analyst but for this job you need a bit of imagination. I don't care if Obbie finds infractions of codes left over from the gold rush days...you can make them up for all I care. You're the investigators. Investigate! Once they've broken a rule...wham, I'll use my contacts and have the police lock her down so tight a pigeon wouldn't want to stop at her place for a shit."

"You're sending me to a brothel?" Obbie queried.

"You're the perfect person. You despise the harlots; none of the girls could tempt you. You'll do it, Obbie."

"Not me," Obbie ardently proclaimed. "Not in a lifetime would I satisfy one of those wenches."

"Gentlemen," Hugh peacefully addressed the

Governor's assistants. "Things are falling into place... perfectly. In fact, what do you say we celebrate?"

He reached into his drawer and took out a bottle of scotch.

The man was indomitable. He had a plan. Misty's was history. Star was on her way out, into a new life, one that Misty had been denying her.

CHAPTER 13: KING FOR A NIGHT

Misty would never know what hit her. In a matter of a week or two, business would cease at the world-famed brothel. The controversy would linger, precluding a reopening until after the election and hopefully subsequent to Star peeking out from the tiny universe she'd resided in since birth—that was the plan.

Hugh Crawford snuggled under the silk sheets next to his wife, cheerily anticipating watching from a short distance the blooming of a girl he adored. All through her upbringing the man had hovered close to her, finding any excuse imaginable to visit Misty's to witness the development of the little star.

Often he'd arrive early in the morning or afternoon when Star was taking dance or music lessons, listening and watching as her skills improved. Misty never objected, even when he'd read books to her as a little girl, play games with her as a bit older girl, and later have chats with her to get to know better what she was learning in her studies or experiencing in her life. She also wasn't adverse to him early on designating himself, "Uncle Hugh."

Clearly, he had made sure he was able to enjoy a tight bond with his girl. She, in turn, had a strong affection for him; the only thing missing was her awareness that Uncle Hugh was really Daddy. He was willing to live with that omission, never addressing whether or not at some point in the future the truth might be revealed either by chance or his intent—or a combination of both.

As he prepared to slip into a sleep state, he laughed out loud. He was imagining Obbie snooping around Misty's. His outburst woke his wife; she had just drifted off.

"What clever misdeed are you drooling over now, my dear?" she posed groggily as she jabbed him playfully in his ribs.

"My little acts of malfeasance over the years have taken care of you quite well, have they not my love?"

"Admitted. I live like a happy princess. And it's all because I married the wisest, smartest, greatest man to ever live," she yawned.

"But you forgot something, best looking?"

"Only when you shave," she teased.

"Then I shall vow to take the razor to my face hourly for the duration of my life," Hugh promised.

"Is that the first lie you've ever told me?"

"Hardly, my princess. I lie to you daily, just to test you."

"Then you should know I've passed with honors. I'm well aware of the boyish yarns you spin. If you haven't noticed, that's how I stay in control of you, by entwining you in your own falsehoods. There's only one fib I better not ever catch you telling me and you know what I'm referring to."

Hugh swallowed. Suddenly his indigestion flared up, causing him to go to the bathroom and chew a Tums. By the time he returned, his wife was blissfully sleeping. Ten minutes passed before the burning sensation subsided.

The truth was he detested his wife. He secretly fantasized about her ensnaring him in an act of infidelity so as to end the sugary charade they carried out daily. There were even times he acted recklessly in hopes she'd uncover his unfaithfulness, lamentably convinced in the end that in truth she lacked the interest in exposing him. Worst of all, he had to admit to himself that he was too uncourageous to take the matter under his own authority and put the old bullet through the relationship's already empty heart.

Obbie making a visit to Misty's: it delighted him anticipating the little saint returning with the goods on The Ranch. The thought permitted him to forget the conjugal admonitions he'd ignored for the past twenty years. He pushed his wife's outstretched arm out of the way and returned to bed. He cuddled close to his foamy pillow, falling swiftly into a dreamy world of fluttering angels dressed in bright white dresses waving sparkling silver wands to bless him.

He awoke refreshed and in a dandy mood.

"You slept well, darling?" his wife asked.

"Splendid. Today is a grand day. You'll be proud to know that your husband is about to take a strong stand on immorality in our wonderful state."

"Oh, is he? What are you going to do, close your hotels and casinos for the day?"

"Bite your tongue, wife," Hugh mirthfully ordered. "I'm declaring war on prostitution, not commerce."

"Prostitution is commerce. I suspect we've been living off it for most of the years—"

"I won't do anything rash, I promise," he snickered, wishing he had a camera to watch as virtuous Obbie stepped foot into Misty's.

It was not until that evening when the hired snoop presented himself at The Ranch. Hugh had instructed Obbie on what to say and made arrangements through a friend for him to be permitted entrance. He had chosen purposefully a show night so that Obbie wouldn't have to be interviewed by Star or Misty, but instead could sit first as a guest to watch the entertainment.

After he'd been admitted into the main room, he would have been seen furtively using his tiny camera to take shots of various violations pertaining to building and safety standards—illegal reconstruction of the building—along with fire code infractions. As he wandered through the facility, he carried a small pad of paper and a pencil, jotting notes to review after he left. He finally put the pad into his breast pocket.

The space was starting to bustle. Obbie was standing alone when a tall blond girl with her hair combed in twin braids dangling almost to the small of her back approached him. Daisy was carrying a platter of appetizers and glasses of champagne, pausing to offer her wares to the guest.

"I'm sure that's all you have to offer," Obbie responded snidely to her solicitous voice.

"Oh, no," she answered sweetly. "I can get you anything you like." Then she hesitated, long enough to inspect him. "You look nervous. Don't worry, we'll take care of you."

"Take care of me?" Obbie scoffed. "I'll bet."

"Well, sir, when you step up to our door looking low, our job is to be sure you leave with a glow."

"My lord! Enough!"

"Oh no. We do love sinfully well," she glowed. "Like pros, we make sure you feel like a King for the Night."

Obbie tried to shut out her message. It was one he'd have never admitted captivated him. Daisy watched while the strange guest squinted as if each word delivered agony.

"It's nice that you came by to give us a try," Daisy added. "We may not be clever, like Albert…whatever, but we sure do know something about love, about satisfying your dreams."

"And how is it you'll determine what my dream is?" Obbie questioned, his sarcasm graduating to contempt.

"Star will figure it out; you'll see," Daisy smiled, indifferent to his hostile attitude.

"Who is Star?"

"She's…wait, you'll see. She's doing a show tonight. You'll love it."

"A show? I presume some sort of erotica to warm up the customers."

"No," Daisy laughed, "Star is the madam. Now be patient," she tenderly instructed, using her right index finger to tap the tip of his nose. Giggling, she took off to serve other clients.

One of the other men that showed up happened to overhear the conversation between Daisy and Obbie. Roy wandered over to introduce himself.

"First time?" he asked, not giving Obbie the opportunity to answer. "Hold on tight. Best experience of your life, guaranteed."

"I've had sex before," Obbie defensively asserted.

"Sure, we all have. For me, hundreds of times," he joked. Then he leaned close to his new friend, whispering to him. "But have you ever been loved?"

"I think so." Obbie was tentative responding, the question shocking him.

"I thought so too. Then I came to Misty's," Roy said reverently.

Obbie couldn't tolerate any more of the discussion. Derisively, he challenged the man standing next to him holding a drink in his hand and a relaxed smile on his face.

"These are filthy whores, for Christ sakes. What does that have to do with love?"

"Tonight you'll find out." Roy slapped him on the back, a buddy gesture not appreciated by Obbie.

His irritation, however, was circumvented as the music went silent, the lights flickered, and a drum roll thundered through the room. Off to the side, a figure emerged. It was a women dressed in a black male suit with a bright red tie. She loped into the room. Then she hopped up on to the small stage set up toward the rear.

The guests all began clapping. Star, appearing like a master of ceremonies, was holding a microphone in hand. She stood in front of the group and bowed. Behind her were two of her girls, Brie, a streamline brunette with the figure of a dancer, and Hollie, a black girl with spiky jet-black hair. As Star turned and waved her arm to point them out, the crowd cheered again.

"Welcome everyone. It's the third Wednesday of the month and we all know what that means—a little pre-entertainment entertainment. Tonight, as a special treat we're presenting...*King for a Night*. That's right," she hollered to arouse the group, "tonight one of you will be crowned...King."

Star now stepped forward and made her way through the all-male audience. She stopped first at a man she seemed well acquainted with.

"Your name? Please sir, so everyone can hear."

"I'm Luke," he giggled, "but you know that. I've only been coming her for twenty years."

"Every day is the beginning of a new life," Star commented merrily. "Now, Luke, if you were king for one night, what would your first wish be?"

"Drive my Porsche in a professional race," he smirked, holding up his keys for everyone to see.

Star pulled a deck of cards out of her jacket pocket and scanned them.

"I'm sorry. Can't do it tonight. But..."

She stopped to look across the room. After making eye contact with Charlotte, a girl with red hair and a faintly freckled face, she motioned for her to come over.

"Say hello to Charlotte," Star suggested as the audience applauded. "She's not a race car but I promise she'll red line your engine. Have fun."

Star then moved on to a man named Armand. While she was addressing him, Brie, and another girl, Allie, on stage, began arranging a king's throne, positioning on the seat a crown and cape.

"Ever been a king, Armand?" Star inquired.

"I've felt like one, but honestly I've never been officially titled."

"What made you feel that way?"

"Surrender," he answered, smirking while looking over at his favorite girl, May.

"My friend, you're lucky to be so easy to please. May is yours for the night." Star stepped back on the stage and pranced across, muttering for everyone to hear. "Surrender. Surrender 'til your heart's content." Then she perked up. "Men, I'm still looking to find me a king."

She inspected the small crowd, this time eyeing Obbie.

"Looks like a newcomer. What's your name?"

"Obbie," he answered flatly.

"Obbie," she repeated slowly, pondering a point. "I'm feeling something. Obbie. Would you like to be a king?"

"I wouldn't," he uttered without emotion.

"Are you sure?" she posed playfully.

"I guarantee it, you can find a better king."

Star rotated to look at Brie and Allie.

"Brie, come over here and tell me if I'm imagining it but I'll swear I see royalty in this face."

Brie waltzed to where Star was with Obbie, carefully inspecting the man who might be crowned. After a few seconds perusing him, Brie's face assumed a look of astonishment. Her hands reflectively reached for her mouth to emphasize the immensity of her discovery.

"I see it too," she finally announced gleefully. She then pointed to Obbie's face. "It's the broad forehead."

"She's right, Allie concurred," having invited herself to take a peek. "I see king all the way."

"Who would have known that in our midst would be a real king," Star said with astonishment.

"You got me all wrong," a flustered Obbie protested.

"Obbie," Star rejoiced. "My girls and I are never wrong about this sort of thing. It's your night; you are going to be," she paused to prolong the moment, then elevated her game show voice, "King for a Night!"

The entire group of customers and staff cheered. The music increased in volume. Brie and Allie ran back on stage and grabbed the large cape, taking it to Obbie and wrapping it around the panicked man's body. Then they lead him on to the stage.

"I'm telling you I'm not a king. I'm not king material," he chanted as if pleading.

Oblivious to his protests, the girls pulled him to the throne and insisted he take his awarded seat. They handed the crown to Star, the onlookers roaring with laughter.

"Obbie, I hereby crown you. You are now officially, King for a Night."

Star was placing the king's crown on his head when Brie started jumping up and down, pointing.

"I think I see a tear."

Hearing Brie exulting, Allie examined the royal one

to see if there was confirmation. Instantly she threw her body wildly, thrilled to announce: "He's a weeper."

Making the absurd situation all the more theatrical was the earnestness of Star, Brie and Allie as they acted out the scene. But even more comically sublime was that Obbie pulled a hanky from his pocket to dab the tears that were trickling from his eyes.

"You got the wrong guy", as if he were daffy the man about to be crowned feebly protested.

The girls began strutting seductively around the sitting king.

"That's a mistake we would never make," Star assured him. "Tonight my good sir, you are king; we're all here to praise, honor and serve you. Oh yes, you are my commander and if you'll just tell me when, where and how, I'll bow."

Star nodded to punctuate her message and then continued. "Can you feel some excitement yet? Being a king is quite the thing...I'll bet. Imagine, you sit alone atop your throne with all the power you've ever known." A grand smile of filled her face. "Come on, show us your royal might. Let me treat you soft and tender now cause you're the lord and the leader, my Caesar, my king."

"Now, king, command me," Star pled. "What's your wish?"

"I wouldn't know where to begin," Obbie squinted, a fresh tear streaming down his cheek. "I've never commanded. I don't have a family. I don't have a girl-friend…it's just me alone."

"So it is with every great king, King Obbie," Star pro-fessed. "Their subjects worship them, often fear them, serve them faithfully, die honoring them but their leader is usually the loneliest soul on earth. You, Obbie, are an honest king, a royal man fearless to say the truth, what most would never admit. For that you are a great king," Star stated solemnly, watching as her words caused a free flowing cascade of liquid from the king's saddened eyes. "Tonight, you will have no pain of isolation or sol-itude, I promise that to you my king."

Toni had been standing in the wings during the cer-emony. When Star spotted her, with her angelic pale face, curly auburn hair and short sturdy body, she had no problem selecting the king's queen. Gently she lifted Obbie off the throne, taking his hand while aiming him toward a couch. She leaned his body backward, motion-ing to Toni that she was to take over.

"Give him…The Treatment," she trumpeted. These two words, as they did each time she spoke them, brought the entire staff of girls to a freeze. Leaving Ob-bie in the tender hands of Toni, Star jumped back on stage to address the audience.

"Come back soon…and don't forget, next time YOU might be King for a Night."

Everybody in the room resumed the activities they were doing before the show began. One by one the girls moved toward Obbie, bowing at his feet and then hugging him. Food and drink was brought to him as he rested his head on Toni's shoulder; even the patrons came to congratulate him.

Misty's upcoming disaster might have spelled doom for the ranch. But Star had mastered her role likely long before even having to step in on an emergency basis. Any potential for failure was snuffed out the minute that Star took over. Helping to keep Misty's at the top of the heap was that there was now a new super chef, reputed by the clientele to even eclipse the prior esteemed genius of tongue. The customers were ecstatic about visiting; delighted to be entertained by the new madam. Everything had fallen blissfully into place...except.

There were two potentially destructive problems insidiously brewing. Hugh was determined to end the party and bring Star out to thrive in what he believed to be the real world. Star had no family roots to cling on to; she had no idea where she came from. Then to further imperil what Misty perceived as a glorious situation, Star had normal female drives, juicing to play games of love.

CHAPTER 14: A PICTURE AND A POST CARD

Deze was a card, a wild hair one might easily dismiss as a "daffy broad." No doubt to some degree that would be an accurate label. But the exterior persona of this lady was highly misleading. While she would be unwittingly entertaining her subjects with her apparent inanity and senselessness, her senses at the same time would be sucking in clues, leads and facts.

After reading one of her stories, the individual about whom the piece was written might deduce that the zany lady had intentionally uncovered them. The perceptions she would include in the article would be frightfully accurate and the material provided to the reporter subsequently researched meticulously. Her articles always received praise, and not infrequently, owing to their candor, created controversy.

Misty's Place

When she left Misty's Ranch after meeting Star for the first time, she set about making random notes. She recalled dwelling on how impressed she was with Star's intelligence, wisdom, poise, culture and etiquette—she was a woman vastly more mature than the not even twenty-years of life she had. At the same time, she recognized that the unimaginably unique circumstances of her life, never having left the ranch, had to raise conflict for the new madam.

The mother was a prostitute.
She died giving birth to Star.
Misty raised the baby at the ranch.
Misty provided for her like a princess.

As Deze mused the situation, it seemed to fit, except she sensed more to the story.

"It's just instinct," she expressed to her boss, Al Plotnick, after she returned to her hotel in Vegas. "I'll need another day here to look into a couple leads."

"I told you not to stay at the Wynn—too expensive."

"I make you so much money. Does Mr. Plotnick ever say, 'Thank you, Deze. I'm so pleased to have you on my staff?' Never. Never. Someday there will be no Deze when you wake up and then you'll cry."

"I can't wait...and don't eat too much."

Plotnick hung up in his typically abrupt manner. It was something that Deze had long before conditioned herself to ignore.

As she jotted down note after note, she kept coming

back to Crystal. The ex-employee obviously had a bond with Star since the lady had been present after she was born and for years subsequent. Plus, she had furtively kept a picture of the young madam's mother, finally sending it for Star as a keepsake.

The information forwarded by Star that afternoon indicated that Crystal had stayed in Vegas after retiring. She lived in Summerlin, a planned community abutting The Red Rock area to the north. It was at most a thirty-minute drive from her hotel. Her plan was to call and see if she could set up an appointment for the following morning, and then catch a flight back home late that afternoon.

Deze was surprised when she reached Crystal. On the other end of the line, she heard yelling and crying in the background.

"Yes, I'm Crystal," the voice strained to compete with the ruckus. "Who are you?"

"I'm a reporter for Play Time Magazine—"

"Yes, I know it," Crystal responded excitedly. "I read it every month."

"Well, I'm Deze—"

"Yes again, how wonderful. I just finished your article, *Fewer Settings for Jet-Setters*. It was excellent."

"Thank you, but the reason I'm calling is to see if I can meet with you. It's about Star."

There was a moment of silence before Crystal

answered. "I'm not sure what you want with me. I prefer not going on records discussing either Misty or Star."

"I just want to ask some questions…I promise that I will not quote you in any article I write. I'll sign a statement to that effect if you would like."

"Okay. When would care to meet?"

"I was planning to leave tomorrow, so if possible in the morning?"

"I don't have a sitter tomorrow, but you're welcome to come to the house…the kids aren't usually this noisy."

They arranged to talk at ten. That evening Deze took dinner alone at the swanky SW Steakhouse at the hotel, and then retired early. She took a walk in the morning and then asked the bellman to hail her a cab. In no time, the driver had exited the freeway and was heading north on Charleston. Deze noticed a sign, *Gala Gourmet Foods*, the thought of something to eat awakening the awareness she'd forgotten to have breakfast.

"Would you mind pulling in there at the market so I can get something? I'll only be a minute," Deze instructed her driver.

Deze loved fine food. Browsing the aisles wetted her appetite. As soon as she spotted tall plastic containers filled with fresh berries and other assorted fruits with yogurt, she knew her breakfast needs were half-filled. She moved on to the bakery section and ordered a bran muffin to go, picking from the bag pieces of the well-baked top on her way to the register.

The total was $11.43; the place was not shameful pricing their products, she mused. Her dinner had been $75.00 with tip. As she tallied the numbers it devilishly thrilled her knowing that when she submitted her expenses, the curmudgeonly Mr. Plotnick would moan as if he were about to declare bankruptcy owing to her "senseless extravagancy"—it was a routine reenacted every time she spent even a dime.

She had just put her wallet back in her purse and was about to exit the door to venture on her mission to see Crystal when by chance she noticed Hampton come in. He was carrying a paper in his hand and his head bore down as he scanned whatever had been written on it.

"Hi, I'm Deze," she shouted sufficiently loud for each of the customers in the front of the store to stare. "You're Hampton, that marvelous maestro of cuisine at Misty's. We met yesterday."

"Yes, of course. I'm here to shop for a few of the items we don't order in," he announced, showing her the list.

"Well, unless the young madam invites me for a dinner, I don't see how I'll ever taste a full meal of yours... of course, I could put on a suit and pass myself off as a man," she gaily chortled. "That Star, oh, what a special one she is. I loved, loved, loved seeing her. You're so lucky to know her."

"I've had surprisingly little contact with her. Then again, I've only been working for her a few months."

Deze moved to close the distance between them,

whispering her grand secret. "I think she's sad. The poor dear lost her mother at birth."

"I don't know anything about her personal life."

Now taking the liberty to push herself close enough that her upper body was leaning into him, she continued. "No lover; no mother."

Then impulsively Deze pulled away from Hampton and reached into her purse. She took out her phone and started fiddling until she produced the image she was looking for.

"Voila!" she spoke as she placed the screen of her phone in front of Hampton. "That's the little lady's mother. I'm going to build that part of Star's past into my story. Tragic, isn't it?"

Hampton casually inspected the picture. His heart skipped a thousand beats in a fraction of a second, but his face gave no clue.

"To lose a parent—especially a mother—so early in life is a tragedy. You've said it well," Hampton expressed. "Now I must tend to my chores. We'll be busy today. Our weekdays are always much more hectic than the weekends."

"Why?"

"Many of our clientele are married and have to spend Friday and Saturday with their spouses," he answered with indifference.

"Well, I hope to see you again. I promise," she winked, "I'll put you in my article.

Deze went back to the cab. They drove several miles. In the distance, the alternating layers of tan and rusty orange of the red rock canyons became visible. Then as they passed on the left a large hotel with the same *Red Rock* name, the Summerlin development came into view. The driver made a right turn and drove about a half mile until he came to the last home on a street that ended at the beginning of a large undeveloped stretch of land.

Deze was hardly out of the car when the front door opened and two blond haired boys, both under five years of age, came running out. They each took one of her hands and started pulling her toward the house. Crystal was watching from the porch, smiling at the behavior of her energetic sons.

"Come in," Crystal greeted. "Nice to meet you. This is Josh," pointing to the larger boy, "and this is Trance. We named him that because we knew from when he was still in my tummy that he was a charmer," she smiled, at the same time tickling him to laughter. "I can imagine what you're thinking."

"You're fortunate. You must have a wonderful husband and you have two amazing sons," Deze stated solemnly. "For Deze, these dreams never came true."

"I'm sorry. I never thought they would for me either, but I really have Misty to thank. You see, she nurtured all of us to become what she saw we could be, what we didn't realize was our potential. I was a college student at

Ohio State University before I started working for her. I had no money and my family...it was horrid. So I started coming to Vegas during the summers to support myself and help my brothers and sisters.

"By chance, I met Misty. She interviewed me for hours, on several occasions, before she hired me—she did that before she took on any of us. That's why she was so successful; she spared nothing when it came to making her clients feel at home and relaxed—she wanted employees she could mold into debutants more than whores. That's why we all stayed for years and when we left we were in the excellent financial shape she promised.

"Misty insisted that we invest half of our earnings in a plan that she managed," Crystal laughed. "She was a financial wizard, I swear. She made us all rich. If not for her, we'd be in the soup now. My husband is a contractor and was badly injured last year. He's had two surgeries and not been able to work—but we're doing fine. We'll, that's my story. Come in. I made some coffee."

They walked through the entrance into a large living space. It was in shockingly good order given that she had two young ones. The walls were covered with family pictures, Deze stopping to look at each one.

"You broke out of it. Look what you did."

"I'm really not doing anything much different than I did then. I came to accept that my purpose was to take care of people. I love it now. I think you have to make

174

peace with your destiny before you can live it fully. If you're fighting it, too much of your self is spent in the battle. I'll go back to thanking Misty. She taught us to have pride in what we were doing…and be the best. I like to think of myself now as the best wife and mother. And yes, my husband knows my past. I just hope my children won't. Not that I'm embarrassed. I don't want to ever have to put them to the test of understanding."

"You're a remarkable woman," Deze complimented.

"No, I'm not. But I am tired," she laughed. "Here I am yakking about me and I didn't even ask what brings you."

"I'm doing an article on Misty's Place, really on Star. She mentioned you in particular and I thought I might pick up from you some of her early history." Deze stopped to rummage through her purse, producing her cell phone again. It was already set to bring up the picture of Star's deceased mother that she had showed to Hampton. She held it up for Crystal to look at. "Star was touched that you sent her the picture."

"It's odd, isn't it," Crystal reflected, "that I didn't take it there myself rather than mailing it? It's less than an hour's drive for me and I've never returned," she stated, seeming puzzled by her reluctance to go back to the ranch. "I can't explain why I won't let myself go back. But yes, I did send the picture. I was cleaning drawers not long ago and came across it."

"You look sad," Deze commented, noticing Crystal's eyes moistening.

"I didn't tell her the whole story. I didn't want to take a chance on hurting Star unnecessarily. I was like a mom to her a lot. If I knew for sure..." She began weeping. "I'll be back in a minute. Please, watch that the boys don't get into trouble."

Crystal was gone less than a minute, returning with a postcard in her hand.

"Take a look at this," Crystal suggested, handing the card that contained only six scribbled words to Deze.

I love you. I miss you.

Deze read the short message, glancing up at Crystal for an explanation.

"There was a terrible fight between Gyps—that's Star's mother's name—and Misty just before Gyps went to the hospital. None of us could ever understand it. Sure, we all had issues with Misty from time to time, like any relationship between a boss and employee. Misty was strict and there was no doubt she had rules that all of us knew not to break. Then there was Gyps; she broke them all, over and over. Misty's tolerance was totally out of character; had any of us done the same thing we would have found our clothes packed and a cab waiting to haul us away.

"Gyps got away with everything. She was like a little sister to us and we all adored her rather than resented the favoritism that she enjoyed from Misty. She was by far the most beautiful of our whole crew. She was also smarter in my opinion than any of us, but her greatest asset was her wisdom about people and life. The girl could see deep into the human character, and she could understand patterns of relationships none of us grasped—but she still managed to screw up in the most idiotic ways, and repeated the same mistakes time and again," Crystal laughed fondly.

"I'm getting off track, aren't I? Well, after the baby was born, Misty came back. I'd never seen her like that. She was devastated. All she said was that Gyps had died giving birth and none of us were to ever mention her name again—there wasn't one of us dumb enough to defy her.

"Of course, we all grieved Gyps. But even before that, I had come up with an idea that I initially brought up to the girls. We knew it would never fly but I became the spokesperson and presented it to Misty. We proposed that we raise the baby at the ranch. You could have laid me under a street paver and I wouldn't have felt it, I was so shocked when, in the end, she agreed.

"A few weeks later, I received that card in my box—we all had our own private mail slots. It's from New York. I know Gyps' writing but this was near illegible. Still, I'll swear it was from her; I just sensed it. I never brought it up to Misty. I never mentioned it to the other girls. I never heard a word after that. It's been almost two decades. Is she alive?" Crystal posed rhetorically.

"Star said you told her not to mention the picture to Misty. Why?"

"I just wanted Star to know she had a mom and to be able to see how gorgeous she was. But if I told her that Gyps might be alive, then I'd be calling Misty a liar. I'd never want to hurt her like that, especially now after her illness. Maybe it's best to just let it die," Crystal said mournfully.

"I think you may have acted wisely. Might it not be worse for Star to know her mother could be alive, but she had never sought out her daughter; and that Star could never find her regardless?"

"If she is alive, there's only one person who might be able to explain the mystery, and that's Misty. She may have concluded that Gyps could have never handled a baby and paid her off to disappear; and then kept paying her to stay away. Gyps was too young and immature to nurture a child. There was part of her I could tell that had been damaged; abused early in her life. Misty is a practical woman—she's also very wealthy and has powerful connections. If she wanted this to go away, she could do it."

Deze left with questions she could never answer and that she could never put in writing. That afternoon she was on a plane, typing the introduction to her article about an extraordinary young madam at Misty's Ranch. She would never solve the riddle of what happened to Gyps. She would, however, serve as a conduit for the mystery to resurface. In fact, she'd already done so but would have had no way of knowing the role she played—Misty's Ranch was destined for multiple crises, and innocent Star had been assigned the role of lead actress in the script.

CHAPTER 15: YOUNG LOVERS

It was early in the morning. Star was alone in the main hall. She was standing on a step stool, extending her body to reach a picture that had tilted. It had been annoying her for days. On the tips of her toes, she was stretching her arms enough so that her fingers could only tap the bottom of the frame to move it. In this most vulnerable position, she heard a voice. The sound registered as belonging to a mature adult, yet she recognized elements of a younger person's tonal quality, those characteristics being ones that resonated as familiar to her.

She allowed her arms to drop down as she glanced in the direction of the young man. He was dressed in a pair of khaki pants and a maroon sport shirt. His hair was rusty brown in color, and wavy; he slicked it back. His mustache had been trimmed neatly, the golden tone shined as his mouth stretched to accommodate a smile that one might interpret as teasing, if there were any known context for his gesture.

In his right hand, he held a bag that he placed on the floor next to him. Noticing that the mysterious object had caught Star's attention served to elongate the mirthful look on his face.

"Can I give you a hand?" he offered, taking a step toward her. "I have a few inches that might help."

"How did you get in here?" Star asked in a demanding tone as she stepped down from the stool.

"I have an executive pass." He offered a slight bow, then reached in his pocket and produced a See's sucker. He held it out to her. "A gift for you."

"How thoughtful. Well, I'm sorry, most of the girls are resting," she curtly informed him, unwittingly unwrapping the sucker and aiming it into her mouth. "Look, if you know what you're interested in, I'll see if I can work something out."

"Actually I'm looking for this amazing madam I read about in a preview for a magazine article."

"I'm she." Star for the first time permitted a sign of humor. "But honestly nobody comes to see me."

"Oh, they don't? Why is that?"

"You going to straighten this picture for me?" Her lightness defied the offense his audacity had earned for the uninvited entrance. She hadn't even addressed how he had gained entry without her knowledge.

The fellow hopped on the stool, easily performing

what Star was laboring to accomplish. He shifted the right lower corner, the piece moving a bit too far and thus still unaligned.

"A tiny bit to the left," Star instructed. "Close…a little more."

Following her order, he all of a sudden pushed opposite and the frame moved significantly to the right.

"Left, I said left," she drilled at him.

He then shifted it left, but far off center. Making matters worse, as he did what appeared to be an intentional act to annoy her, he smirked.

"Oh, you're a great help," she scolded.

"I'm a slow learner," he responded slowly, allowing his statement to register with his subject. He then took a single leap, landing on the floor, staring at her. "Now, why is it nobody comes to see you?

"I'm like a vendor or artisan of fine merchandise. They want what I have to sell but could care less about me."

"Well, I'm not here for the product. I never wanted it."

His words tweaked her attention. She examined his face. Then in an instant, an expression of shock came over her. There was a faint recognition she couldn't help but process. As she stood gazing at him, he reached for the sack he had put on the floor. He took out a pair of riding boots and stood holding them up for her to see.

"I'm Justin. I guess I'm the only customer that never spent a dime at Misty's."

"Finally, after all this time," she beamed, the joy irrepressible as witnessed by her freely waving the candy stick she had been suckling on. "Finally, I get my boots back. It's been about seven years. With interest, a late return penalty and a restocking fee, you owe me...you owe me more than you can afford, my friend."

"What if I just come back for one of those riding lessons and see if you don't kill me this time?"

"Well, you are the worst learner I've ever seen."

"And you're the worst teacher," he laughed, Star joining in the merry mood. "That's the only reason I never forgot you. Somewhere in the back of my head, no matter where I went or what I was doing, I always remembered—"

"That twelve-year-old who told you about relaxation engineers."

"Exactly."

"Even I couldn't have believed it anymore."

Justin peered into Star's eyes, beholding a woman even more beautiful than the fantasies he'd created over the years.

"I was sure you'd have forgotten me after...well, it's been a while, hasn't it?"

"How could I forget you? I've never seen anyone else pass up one of Misty's girls."

"I was just cheap," he joked.

As Justin was testing her emotions, and Star was battling to keep them light, Daisy came in.

"Shall I bring in the girls, Star?" she asked, glancing at the handsome man talking to her boss.

"No, Daisy. I'll take care of this one myself."

Daisy started to leave, nearly unable to swallow a silly thrilling grin.

"Misty asked me to tell you that when you have time she needs you in the office."

"Tell her I'll be there soon, please."

"How is Misty?" Justin asked as Daisy closed the door.

"She's as good as she's going to get...let's just say she'll never be the same but she's doing well. Still, she couldn't handle things here, so I had to take over. Tell me, what have you been up to all these years?"

"Let's see...college back east, graduate school in London, a consulting position I hated in Boston...and now I'm here...without a job in the world. You wouldn't by chance have something for me at the ranch?"

"You couldn't even straighten a picture," she playfully mocked. "I don't think you'd be qualified to rustle cattle. But I'll give it some thought while I'm helping Misty."

"What do you think about me coming back later this week to find out?" he proposed.

"Come back and we'll talk."

"You've been with me all these years, Star. I wanted—"

"Come soon, okay?"

184

She walked toward the door to signal that it was time to leave. As quickly as he cleared the threshold, she took a deep breath, holding it for an unimaginable length of time. As she exhaled, she couldn't repress the thoughts elbowing their way into her mind's eye.

Had he remembered her the same as she had him? Did he hold all those years in his heart a sweet spot for her, as she had for him? Did his body experience strange sensations when he thought about her, as her body did when she recalled her time with him? Did he want her as she had always dreamed having him?

It was a parade, questions that presented themselves like floats, orchestras and marching bands followed by horses with riders, all cruising down the thoroughfare of her mind. It was all in her imagination but seemed so real.

The drums beat and the horns blew, the stallions strutted, while high atop the riders smiled and waved; beautiful flowers camouflaged vehicles where lovely young girls stood gleefully in skimpy outfits. It was New Year's Day, Christmas, Thanksgiving, Easter Day, Fourth of July, and best of all, Valentine's Day, all in one. The effect had caused her to do what she rarely did, sweat.

She sat down, too overwhelmed to stay afoot. It was then that the unexpected happened. The streamers of bright colors suddenly fell from the sky and were littering the ground. The rose, gladiola, tulip and daisy petals browned and wilted. The feisty, lively and energetic sounds of music were replaced by screeching, deafening voices, foreboding and terrifying.

Star shuddered. The fantasy imagery now was composed of swords, muskets and steel suits that had been hauled out of storage, arming her for a battle against an ancient foe. Something had to be killed; the fragrance of those robust flowers she'd smelled moments before was now a sickening, noxious stench of death.

Murder. Murder. Murder.

She heard the word shouting its way up the queue like a cheat, having printed itself on a banner three times in red letters.

Murder. Murder. Murder.

Then the finale: *Kill love!*

Those final words left her trembling. When her mind finally cleared of the powerful visuals that had invaded her mental being like a waking nightmare…she wept. Was she ordering the execution or was it beyond her authority where the command was authored? Was the scene that had played out in her mind been nothing other than pathetic nonsense, an invention she had birthed from no more than inglorious fear?

Sobbing, Star never heard the sound of a door opening. It was behind the bar. The hinges had been well greased so that as the wood swung soundlessly, the motion of the object was as inaudible as the idling motor of a hybrid car. Hampton had come to inspect the supply of lemons and limes under the counter. He noticed the weeping young lady, staring momentarily before silently closing the door as he exited to leave her to her privacy.

Misty was going to have to wait in her office for Star this time; the young madam had suffered a minor stroke of her own.

CHAPTER 16: HOW LUCKY CAN YOU GET?

Hampton was off every Saturday and Wednesday. He had his own quarters on the ranch and typically he'd stay Saturdays to oversee his staff. But every Wednesday he'd take off to the city, religiously visiting the girl he now considered his adopted daughter. Her name was Rose.

She remained living in the same location where they had been together beneath the moral depravity and hypocritical glitz of the gambling capital of the universe. They'd usually walk to a park and talk, sometimes stopping for Hampton to treat her to a meal.

Shortly before Deze's shocking chance encounter with Hampton, he had been with Rose. When he saw her, he immediately recognized a change, though he couldn't imagine what had happened. She was always quiet and her emotions had remained fragile. But now he sensed a distance he couldn't compute.

He tried to pry subtly, making sure he wasn't being intrusive. She was wired tight. Whatever it was he sensed, alarmed him. If anything, as the months had passed since he took the job at Misty's, she seemed to be coming out gradually and he had hoped that a mending of her soul was underway. Now, watching her stare mindlessly at her food alarmed him.

He left to return to his job with his curiosity unsatisfied. He worried about her for the next several days, deliberating if he should leave on his next day off to try and talk with her again: he decided it might startle her and reasoned he'd wait until the next Wednesday. Then after the unexpected meeting at the store with Deze— seeing the picture of Star's mother and realizing it was his own Rose that had birthed his new employer—he couldn't wait for his day off. He didn't know how he was going to handle it, not even sure what the "it" was that might need his attention.

By then he knew that Rose was actually Gyps. He also assumed that the despair that had gripped giant tentacles around her neck and was squeezing the life out of her was due to her failure to take a role in the life of her daughter. It was no different than the tragedy of his life with his own girl, an event of epic proportion that had shattered his world. What he had no reason to conclude was that what he had observed in terms of a change in Gyps related to Star.

It couldn't...could it? He mused.

When the next Wednesday finally came, Hampton dressed eagerly. Then, earlier than normal, he left to meet with her. Armed with the awareness unwittingly bestowed on him by Deze, he planned to probe for the first time to ascertain from her what issues had driven her to the lifestyle she was choosing. To his surprise, and despair, she was gone. It was apparent that she'd abandoned the home she had dwelled in with him because the small case she'd kept under her bed was missing—typically when she went out she'd take her money, but never the case.

He wandered the tunnels for miles. He talked to every person he could find to get a lead where a lady named Rose might have gone. It was a futile exercise. He knew it. The girl never communicated with anyone other than him. Nobody would have known her name.

When he ascended from beneath, he immediately went to the office of the Las Vegas Sun News, inquiring about any unidentified victims of violent crime that might have been found. Then he went to the local police office, similarly exploring any reported incidents. Relieved that it was unlikely she had been murdered or raped, he found himself disturbed by another thought. What if she took off and he'd never see her again? *She left her daughter and never came back. Would she do the same to me,* he wondered?

Each day thereafter whenever he had a break, even dismissing his need for rest, he'd search for her in all the places he suspected he might run into her. His efforts were fruitless; daily he'd return grief-stricken to Misty's. Would he ever see her again? He couldn't stop asking himself. She was a vital part of him, no different than a heart or lung; he was aching both due to her absence as well as the uncertainly about where she might have gone.

Where was Gyps? She was alive. Hampton had perceived accurately that something had changed when he last visited with her. He could have never guessed what had happened; it was a one-in-fifty-million-times-a-billion chance event that accounted for her absence, having nothing to do with Star.

After Hampton took the position at Misty's, Gyps went about her reclusive lifestyle. She never interacted with anyone other than if she were engaged in one of the activities Hampton had taught her regarding how to raise money. From the onset, she was extremely successful, permitting her to always refuse his offers to help her with funds.

She knew how to brush through every casino in town and never catch the attention of guards or the cameras she was aware were watching the guests from every angle and location. It was a rule that she'd never go to the same hotel more than once every two weeks and she was constantly changing her wardrobe. She'd typically wear loose fit clothing to disguise her figure and pull her hair beneath a cap or hat. She'd dress casually and neatly.

One afternoon she was at the MGM Grand Hotel. She had been standing at one of the lively crap tables, by intent next to a man who had just begun rolling. It was near five o'clock, a perfect time in that many of the gamblers liked to try their luck before an evening of gluttony, after which they could come back and play the games again.

This gentleman couldn't roll a seven if his life depended on it. The bets were doubling, tripling and quadrupling. The pit bosses were calling their bosses and they were on the phone with the corporate directors for instructions on how to teach this lunatic that there were more ways to toss a seven than any other number: six out of thirty-six possible rolls to be exact. That's a one sixth chance on each roll. If the man throws six times, the odds are he'll have hit a seven. But this fool must have thrown over a hundred times, never a "crap out" seven; he was becoming a thorn in the side of this desert palace.

Gyps stood cheering: by that time she knew the game and understood what he was doing was unprecedented. Each time before he picked up the two dice to finger them, prior to throwing he'd smile at her, and then yell out for the rest of the tipsy crowd to hear: "This is the girl I've been looking a lifetime for." If it was Gyps doing a magic trick, then he was correct about the lifetime business; the spree he was enjoying was approaching odds outside the bounds of probability for any human.

Rituals are born quickly when unusual circumstances confront man. In this case, Gyps, before the man picked up the dice, would signal with a nod at the precise moment he was to go ahead and roll. However, on this particular toss, as the gambler was about to reach for the pair of squares that had been stick-shoved across the table to rest in front of him, Gyps, instead of giving him the go-ahead sign, turned and walked away. The man was startled...too fearful to throw.

"Take me down and cash me in," he shouted to the team of croupiers and boss men, each smiling delightfully at the thought of him taking his cursed luck with him.

He raced after Gyps. She had moved swiftly. Quickly, she was out the door. He caught sight of her red knit cap about to disappear into the swarm of people walking along the street.

"Was it over?" he asked anxiously as he raced alongside of her.

Gyps stared at the man mutely.

"You didn't tell me to keep rolling. Did you know it was over?"

"No. I was bored," she answered dispassionately.

"I made a fortune. I'm getting out of here tonight. Can I see you before I leave?"

"No," she said flatly. "You don't want to know me. Good luck."

She turned to leave but again he pulled at her, this time placing in her hand a ticket.

"Take this. I bought it earlier today. It's a California lottery ticket. I buy one every time I come to Vegas, before I leave home in San Francisco. After I return home a loser from Vegas, I check to see if I've won back my losses," he chuckled. "Damndest thing but they won't allow the lottery in Nevada. Anyway, it's my tradition though I've never seen a penny return—good luck to you, and thanks."

He went back to the casino. Gyps unmindfully placed the piece of paper in her pocket.

"Suckers, they're all helpless fools," she muttered as she dissolved once more into the nothingness she had come to appreciate.

The following day she wore the same jacket. She reached into the pocket and felt a piece of paper, pulling out the lottery ticket she had forgotten she'd placed there. The absurdity of gambling inclined her to toss it on the street. But instead, being in a fair mood, she let down her guard enough for curiosity to sneak up on her, sufficiently to permit serendipity's allure to grab her with its mighty talons.

A half hour later, she picked up a copy of the Los

Angeles Times at a 7-Eleven convenience store. She asked the clerk where to find the lotto results. He was wearing a turban on his head and spoke with an Indian accent.

"You want to win? I wish you most luck, lady." He was joyous, as if eager for a celebration. "Let me see your ticket," he kindly offered, opening the newspaper to the proper page.

He scanned carefully, double and then triple checking to be sure. Each time he read the numbers, his eyes widening. The glee split his lips to the point where his excitement became agonizing to watch.

"One hundred twenty-nine million dollars," he whispered, unable to raise the volume of his voice. Gyps was the only customer in the store. She grabbed the ticket and the paper and ran out, continuing at full speed until she was out of the man's sight.

Gyps sped to her home as quickly as her legs would move. She reviewed the paper to be sure the man wasn't mistaken or using her for a cruel hoax. For two days straight she didn't leave, deliberating what to do. The thought of luck of such an enormous improbability frightened her, more accurately terrified her. She seriously entertained swallowing the evidence to defy an act of destiny she knew would have to dramatically alter her life. She also wondered if she might claim the money and then pay no attention to it ever again—she'd read stories of vagrants who die and later had discovered by heirs that they were worth a fortune.

She finally opted to take the money, but with conditions. What she needed was an attorney. She took a bus to downtown Las Vegas. Randomly she chose an office building and scanned the directory for a lawyer. The building was full of them. Her eye flitted along the lines reading names like Antonio, Del Rio, Winston, Peck, Bixby and Sabath. Then she noticed the name Rothman, Abraham Rothman, Suite 2811.

She recalled from childhood hearing her father ranting in a drunkin' rage about "the cheap Jew bastards," and how "the goddamn Jews run the world economy." That was good enough for her. Comforted that she wouldn't have to ask Mr. Rothman if he was Jewish, she went to the elevator and pressed the number twenty-eight.

She entered the reception area.

"Is Mr. Rothman in?" she inquired.

"Yes, but he only consults by appointment," the secretary softly informed the plain appearing woman standing opposite her.

"Well, I believe he'd find my situation of interest. If you want to tell him, please, I'm prepared to pay whatever his fee is for a meeting immediately."

"Really, I'm sorry but I've been instructed not to accept walk-in business," the woman replied firmly.

Gyps turned to leave. She opened the door and went out to the hallway. As she turned right to make her way back to the elevators, she noticed a door open that she assumed was part of Rothman's suite. A grey haired gentleman with a friendly face walked out, smiling as Gyps approached.

"By chance, are you attorney Rothman?" she queried.

"Yes, I am. Can I help you, dear?"

"Your secretary told me that you don't take clients without an appointment. I'm wondering if you might make an exception."

Rothman examined the beseeching features of her face, the beauty blemished by unmistakable agony. "It would be my pleasure," he kindly greeted her, reaching out to shake her hand. "Would you mind if I went to the men's room first? I'll come get you as soon as I return if you'll wait for me in the reception area."

Rothman was a squat man wearing a black suit with royal blue tie, his belly protruding but not offensively. It was not five minutes before he invited Gyps to follow him to his office.

"I have to assume that you have something important to discuss with me. I'm all yours," he remarked as they walked down the short interior hallway.

Entering the office, Gyps laughed. She immediately noticed through the full glass windows a view of the giant buildings comprising The Strip. She was thinking how distinctly different it was seeing the structures from an elevated perspective rather than from below them. It further tickled her knowing that in a few moments the man whose office she just entered would come to understand that if she wished, she might buy the building.

"I'm delighted to have a paying customer show up unexpectedly because I had the honor of taking my wife out last night for our anniversary," he joked. "I shouldn't be teasing, should I? And please, this consultation is no charge. If we agree to go further, then we'll talk about fees." He shoved a large file on his desk to the side. "So what can I do for you?" he finally asked.

Gyps stood and took out the small ticket, reaching out to let it float on to the space in front of him. He picked up his glasses and inspected it.

"It's a long story, sir, but I'm told by a man at a 7-Eleven store that this ticket is worth over one hundred twenty-nine million dollars."

The office was cluttered. All around the perimeter were huge files on the floor, on tables, and in drawers that were pulled out; there was narrowly room to move. Rothman rose from his chair and walked to the front of the desk, leaning his buttocks against it while staring at the wealthy woman who had obviously mistaken coming to his office.

"I'm happy for you. Certainly you'll be in need of many professionals to help you manage your fortune, but I don't believe I can assist you. I'm a labor attorney. I represent half of the hotels in this city. I'd love to counsel you but I don't handle securities or financial

contracts. Let me refer you to someone who can help...
and congratulations."

Rothman then went back to his seat, picking up the
phone. "I'll take care of this for you right now, Ms.—"

"Mr. Rothman, you don't need to call anyone for me.
You'll be able to handle the matter quite well."

"Then I don't understand."

"All I request of you is to not ask any personal questions about me. I'll give you my name but I don't want it
repeated outside this office. Is that agreed?"

"I don't do assassinations for hire, though I've considered murdering a few of my clients. What is it you
want?"

"I want you to claim the money for me and protect
my identity. I don't want anyone knowing who I am or
that I have a nickel. I want accounts set up where the
money can be secured. Pretend you won it and want it
kept a secret. Do as you would under that condition for
me."

"I understand."

"I don't want to meet the bankers, the agents for the
government, the hotel executives—I don't want to even
think about my name or a picture of me ever being associated with this. All I want is confidentiality."

He stared at the ticket, recognizing it as a California
lottery.

"I happen to hold a California license as well; my firm
in fact has offices in Los Angeles and San Francisco. Just

hold on a minute, please." Rothman pressed the buzzer on his phone. "Edie, get me Trimble in L.A." After a brief wait he continued. "Paul, I have an unusual situation here. I'll be representing a young lady with one hundred twenty-nine million dollars winnings from a lotto game. No publicity on this. Have our people in contracts ready to meet with me tomorrow. I'll be coming in this evening."

Rothman sat listening to Trimble, closing his eyes as he leaned back in his chair. "Tell them nothing except I'm representing the party claiming the money. They don't need to know anything else at this time."

"I'm going to need your name, social security number and some information about what you want to do with the money," Rothman informed Gyps after hanging up from his associate. "I'll have all the papers drawn up later to secure your privacy. We won't need to bring the IRS people in, they'll be there with their hands out before you take a dime."

"My name is Gentry Collier. My social security number is 530-20-7766. As far as the money goes, what do you suggest?"

"Ms. Collier, even after taxes it's a fortune. You have a choice with these lottery winnings. Either you can take a lump sum now or spread—"

"Now. I want it all at one time. Let them take out the taxes," she resolutely informed him.

"You're still going to need professional advice—"

"I'm asking you where I can put it. I live simply and I don't plan on that changing. I don't need it and I don't care much about it. It's already giving me a bad feeling, but I want to think more about it before I decide how to dispose of it."

"Then I'd suggest a brokerage account, with the money invested in U. S. Treasuries."

"That's fine."

"Also, I want a will and trust made out."

"I don't do that personally but—"

"I told you, I don't want to deal with anyone else. It'll be very simple. If you could have one of your colleagues draw it up, that'll be fine. I'll call you later today with the details of what I want it to say."

"You're an interesting lady."

"I'm not even close to interesting," she retorted with an odd sense of nothingness that tweaked Rothman's attention.

"Well, if you don't mind my saying it, you're a beautiful woman and I hope this good fortune that has come your way will help you to better your life."

"I know most people would do anything to change places with me, and might envy my position, but I find this experience unnerving, a dreadful inconvenience."

"I'll pray for you that as time passes you'll be able to adjust better to this circumstance. I do understand if it's of any consolation that an event of this magnitude can be shocking. Give it some time," Rothman advised paternally.

"I'll call you later today. Obviously, you can take your fee out when the money comes."

"Stop by tomorrow afternoon...don't you want to know what my charges are?"

Gyps stood up, smiling at the question they both knew was ridiculous. She left without speaking another word.

The following afternoon, she met with Rothman. He had all the documentation prepared for signatures. It was agreed he'd keep copies of her records secured in his office, along with her will and trust.

Rothman would hear from her shortly.

It wasn't the money that was paining her when she had last met with Hampton. What troubled her was having won. She perceived it as a wicked and perverse punishment inflicted on her to further torture her already suffering soul; a sure curse, ratcheting up the severity of the sentence she had been delivered years before after she'd walked out on her baby.

Yet there was more to her agony. The money, along with Hampton's periodic casual disclosures about Misty's when they would meet—including his occasional comments about the gracefulness of the young madam, Star, and the unfortunate impairing stroke for the older madam, Misty—had awakened an instinct not dissimilar to what Hugh Crawford, the father of her infant, was struggling with and was attempting to overcome.

Her urge to see her daughter became stronger and stronger. In fact, had she not won the money, it had been her plan prior to that to talk with Hampton in cryptic terms about whether or not he thought she could deal with a challenging emotional encounter. Rather than quashing her thirst to complete the mission, somehow her newly acquired wealth had intensified it.

During the two days she stayed sequestered in her underworld abode, the emotional pain she was experiencing reached new heights. No matter how she turned and twisted the fate she had been assigned, it ached her mind, body and spirit unendurably. From the depth of her despair, she found a solution, what she was sure would be an escape from the torment—she finally figured out a plan that would allow her to at last reach out with love to those for whom she cared for most.

She left home and went immediately to the leasing office for the exclusive Turnberry Towers. She took a six-month commitment on a vacant unit offering her a full view of the city; she moved in that day. She then went on a shopping spree, showing up at the most fashionable boutiques in town. The parcels were numerous and she suggested they be delivered to her condo. Next she called to place an order for a week's supply of food to be sent to her new home.

She sat back that evening on the sofa in her living

room, spending the remaining hours of darkness admiring the sparkling, glowing and glittering of the Vegas skyline; she fell asleep as the sun was breaking the horizon in front of her. She smiled as she was drifting off into a refreshing rest.

She thought of herself as a debutante, coming out to be introduced to society.

If the Goddess of Fate had a sense of humor, this was setting up to be a sick display of it.

While Gyps was beginning to make up for the time she lost living like a rat in a sewer, her ex-client and the papa to her daughter, Hugh, was awaiting the go-ahead from Obbie to shut down Misty's. In fact, he'd left a message at the governor's office for Obbie and Walt to come over as soon as they arrived the morning after Obbie visited Misty's. It was shortly after nine in the morning when his secretary buzzed, asking if her boss was ready to meet with the assistants to the state leader.

"You bet. Send the short nerdy one in alone."

As Obbie entered, it was apparent that his stride was more relaxed and confident. He was carrying a stack of papers in one hand and what looked like an article downloaded from the internet in the other.

"So, what good news do you have for me," Hugh asked gaily.

"The latest poll figures...not good," Obbie began. "The governor is dropping support in the Reno-Tahoe area but is about the same in every other region."

"Well, take care of that," Hugh abruptly reacted. "I'm talking about Misty's."

"It was a lot different than I thought," he answered meekly.

"I'll admit, there's not a house like hers in the state... not really anything close to it in the world." Hugh rubbed his hands eagerly. "So, the report, young man. What do you have?"

"Nothing."

"For Christ sakes, Obbie, do not screw with me. I'm not the man you want to toy with."

"I'm wouldn't do that, sir. Here, look at this."

Obbie handed Hugh the printed article. It was actually an excerpt from the upcoming full publication.

"Play Time Magazine! What is this trash?"

"Mr. Crawford. Just look it over," Obbie suggested.

Hugh browsed the pages before reading out loud.

Madam Love by Deze Pinot. He pronounced the last letter with a hard "t," making a mess of her name. "Madam Love!! Who the hell is that supposed to be?"

"The madam; her name is, Star. The story will be released in full next month, but this is a lead to entice people to buy the magazine. Read it, sir."

> *Expecting every imaginable expression of sex and sin, I was shocked to discover that little was to be found. The beautiful madam, Star, had a purity and innocence that gives an entirely new meaning to the word brothel. Her*

205

> *establishment reminded me more of an execu-*
> *tive country club than a…*

Hugh hurled the pages randomly in the air. "Please, God, tell me I'm not going mad." He then glared at Obbie, slowly delivering his next statement. "Obbie, you are worthless. Leave! Now! Do it before I slay you right here. Don't ever mention this to me again."

Hugh stood and pointed toward the door to make his point.

"But—"

"Out. Out. Out with you!!"

Picking up the article off the floor, Obbie dashed for the door. Hugh yelled to his secretary.

"Lisa, send the other one in."

Hugh sat down to compose himself; a second later Walt entered.

"Notice a change in Obbie?" he said, greeting Walt.

"I do. I asked him what happened but he wouldn't say a word."

"The little worm turned on me," Hugh sneered. "It's obvious that Misty's gave him a taste of…you know what. All that hard talk on prostitution, forget about it. My best guess is I just paid for his first visit to the fur factory."

"I always wondered about him," Walt roared with laughter. "I'll bet it was his first time."

"Next time, it's his dime. Now, Walt, I'm making this my number one priority. Without the governor in his position I stand to lose millions, even a billion. Do you understand? Go to Misty's, get her closed down, and keep that zipper of yours zipped."

"Sir, for me, nothing ever gets in the way of business."

"Don't be so sure, cowboy. You've never been to this place. Walking out of there with anything on straight may be the hardest thing you'll ever do. You handle this for me though and I'll tell you what I'm going to do. Get excited! I'm going to bring you aboard as my right-hand man. Walt, any person next to me lives a life you know nothing about. Power, respect, wealth...they're yours. That gets the juices flowing, huh? It'd have me frolicking around here like a horny teen. Ah, lad, have you ever had, *The Feeling of Almost*?"

"I'm not quite sure what you're referring to, unless you mean losing an erection," Walt quipped.

"I have something entirely different in mind," Hugh cunningly replied. Then he twitched his head, as if distracted by a sound or sensation. "Can you fell that little kick? It can pick you up a little quick, and it can make you wanna start to boast...ah, that's the feeling of almost. Startin' to get the picture? Listen," Hugh urged as he moved close to Walt, whispering in his ear. "Don't you love that little thump, it'll get your heart to pump. And, it'll start to make you so engrossed...that's the power of almost—power, young man, power!" Hugh roared as he pulled back from Walt.

"There's more to the story, lad. That feeling, the one

you're getting now, that feeling is right. You're getting close, my friend, but sit tight…'cause what you're getting now is but a slice, but what you're getting is awful nice, righto? Can you see right ahead, so sweet inside your head? That's the golden prize, imagine it before your eyes."

Hugh was near entranced, now motoring around the office in a most uncharacteristic manner. "I know you're on the brink, but push on until the end. Yeah, so I urge you to keep on pushing all the way to the post, because it's so much better than going…almost."

"I think I see where you're headed," Walt commented, but still a measure tentative.

"Now is your chance."

"And I won't pass it up," Walt assured him, pausing to cock his head as if he was now receiving a subliminal message. "I'm sitting close indeed, and things are bright. Is that the feeling of almost? If so, I can't wait until I get a flight." Walt now nodded his head to punctuate his next statement. "I've got a bundle of thrill beneath my chest. I know it, that's the feeling of almost…I can't wait until I feel the rest," he voiced excitedly.

"Are you ready to do battle, my man?" Hugh charmed his new partner.

"Consider it over, sir. There is no…almost with me. When I set out to do a job, I finish it," Walt declared. "I get it! That almost is worthless without getting the rest, the feeling of finishing the task."

"That's what I want to hear. You're a man cut from the same cloth as I."

It was true; both men shared a determination to accomplish whatever task was put in front of them. Powerful men are like that, willing to crush the opposition by any imaginable means, break the rules, redefine the meaning of honor and integrity and slaughter anyone or anything getting in their way. Typically they have only one weakness...sex.

CHAPTER 17: THE BUDDING ROMANCE

The day after Justin left he phoned Star, arranging to see her two days later. Her resolve to murder the potential she recognized for romance creeping into her life for the first time was weak. In spite of all the agitating she had done after he left, she couldn't wait to hear from him again, and then to see him.

On the morning that he was expected, she was in the main hall. She was playing songs from a musical she loved called, *Wrapped*. She was gyrating to the tender rhythm, singing along with the lyrics.

> *Every moment lives forever, every minute lasts 'til never, every hour's like a year and every day is packed with tears.*

On the wall was a mirror. As she swung herself

gracefully around the room, she paused to inspect her appearance. She was wearing a yellow tight-fit top and black slacks. Her hair was pulled back and then tied in a long single braid hanging down to the shoulder level. Around her neck was a gold necklace with a heart pendant that Hugh had given her for her last birthday. Dangling from her ears were long sliver-thin gold leaves.

She straightened her top, making sure the "V" was perfectly centered between her breasts. Her tanned skin glowed from the application of a cream and the scent of her perfume left a subtle residue of lime; she could smell it herself. Her face looked tentative and she couldn't help a short pep talk.

Relax. What are you so afraid of? She spoke to the figure in the mirror.

She had more to say but she was interrupted by a knock on the door.

"Sorry to bother you, Star," Daisy called out above the music, "but you have a visitor."

"Good. You can send Justin in." The breezy manner Star used to instruct her was sure to arouse a reaction of giggling, and then scandalous gossip between the girls.

She remained poised for an additional period, further inspecting the nervousness she couldn't wipe clean from her face. When she heard a rapping sound on the door, she steadied herself before walking to open it.

"Hello, my friend," she greeted him, the forced casualness damning to her. "Can I get you something to make your stay at Misty's more enjoyable?" she asked comically.

"How about a glass of water."

"Sounds about right for you."

"Are you saying I'm a bore already?"

"I'm sure all your lady friends don't see you that way."

"I only have one lady friend," Justin smiled. "Now that I have you in my life, I only need one."

Star swallowed. The emotions stirring were like extraterrestrial creatures, foreign entities she had no idea how to communicate with. The great madam, the confident and self-assured woman writing prescriptions for men's sex fantasies as easily as a chemist the formula for an experiment, recognized she was being sacked by feelings most girls her age had mastered by junior high school. She felt the sensation of nakedness, her mind muddling. She went to get a glass at the bar. As she did, Justin explored the room.

There was a small table next to a couch, an open bound booklet face down suggesting Star had been reading it. While Star was attending to drinks for both of them, Justin picked up the book and began perusing it. When she arrived holding a glass in each hand, she quickly put them down on the table. She then reached abruptly to attempt snatching the material from Justin's hands.

"Off limits," she decried as she grabbed the document.

"Off limits?" Justin objected, refusing to loosen his grip.

"Just give it to me," she insisted with greater authority.

Mischievously he began reading, rotating circularly as Star tried to reach around him to take possession of the material. Justin playfully defended his position. He seemed to be engrossed in the writing.

"Wait a minute. This is very intriguing," he nodded.

"Well, it's not yours."

"This guy, Monty...I think it's clear that his intentions are dishonorable."

"If you don't give that back," she threatened with a shout, forcing Justin to finally hand it over to her.

"I can see that whoever raised you forgot to teach you manners," she chastened.

"You wrote it, didn't you?"

"Doesn't matter," she bantered. "You'll never see it again."

"Why be so mean?"

"You, my friend, deserve it. But yes, I wrote the script."

"A play?"

"Yes. I've always dreamed of being a theatre actress, so I wrote a play for me to act in."

"Well then, since I can't look at it, do me the honor of acting a bit of it for me," he suggested.

"I have a better idea, then," she proposed. "I'll act a bit of it with you, if you're up to the challenge."

She tossed him the script.

"There. Are you happy?"

"Yes. I feel like we're two kids playing together. I'm happy."

"You're impossible. Here I am, one minute promising you'll never see it again and the next asking you to act it out with me. I mean, are you happy you got me to lie?"

"That's not even a lie. It's a change of heart," Justin laughed.

"You leave my heart out of this," she countered wittily.

"Do you believe that's possible? To leave your heart out?"

Star reached into a drawer where there was a second copy of her work.

"Page twenty," she called out, sensing an urgency to alter the course of the conversation. "You can be Monty; I'll be Remy."

"What's the scene about?"

"All you need to know is that my character, Remy, is in love with her brother's closest friend. She'll do anything to get noticed by him."

"A love story?"

"More of a comedy. He hardly gives her the time of day. Still, as he rejects her she deludes herself with the loony idea that he can be hers."

"Okay. I'll try it. I'll need a couple minutes to put on my Monte face." Justin smiled.

He walked to the other side of the room, scanning

the pages. Star sat on a rug, her legs outstretched as she leaned forward with a pencil to scribble notes as if doing homework. Then she stood in the center of the room. Justin strolled over to her. He altered his facial expressions to build the impression of his character, exactly as he imagined he'd play it in a real stage presentation.

"Remy, go get your brother," Monty ordered her gruffly.

"What's your hurry?" Remy asked, intentionally positioning herself to stand directly in front of the boy she had eyes for.

Monte slouched back in a chair, grabbed a magazine, and while they were talking refused to lift his eyes to make contact with her.

"Remy stop being a brat and get him. Your brother and I have two gorgeous dates tonight, beauties! Wonderful, voluptuous—"

"Okay, I get it," she pouted. Then in a sensual manner she added, "I thought you were taking me out tonight."

"You wish...now go get your brother."

"What if I told you," she posed in a seductive voice she'd practiced that afternoon, "I do wish it?" She then crawled on all fours and craned her neck up to try and force a glance by him.

"Then I'd tell you I don't go out with little twerp sisters of my best friend," Monte muttered, looking at the picture of the latest Ferrari racecar.

"But think about this," she persisted, still in an

alluring voice. "What if you used all of your massive, burly power to for one moment forget everything you know about me? Then at that exact instant, you looked up at me? You think then I'd be just a little twerp sister?"

He barely glanced her way, quickly going back to review a picture of the New York Giants Super Bowl winning football team. "Definitely."

"If you weren't so afraid you'd actually take a good look." Remy now stood. She posed herself in front of him. She put her hands on her hips and placed her left foot forward while pushing her weight on the rear right foot, permitting her to promote her blooming breasts to him. "If you looked you wouldn't need to use that fancy imagination of yours."

For the first time, Monte lifted his head to stare at her. He lingered for a moment, the script falling to his lap.

"Oh my God," he whispered as if in a trance. He started to get up, the script now falling to the floor. His eyes were locked on hers. "You're right. I like what I see; I really do," he panted.

Jolted out of her role of Remy, Star put her hands indignantly on her hips.

"What are you doing? That is not what it says and you know it."

"I don't know what you're talking about," he argued. He then picked up the script and pointed randomly. "It is right there," he smirked.

"Stop it!"

He continued pointing. "No. I think you're mistaken. It's somewhere...let me find it." He searched by flipping wildly through the pages.

"No, it's nowhere. You, my friend, made it up."

"No, you got the story wrong," he humored.

"It's my story! How can I get it wrong?" she chuckled, permitting the exchange to become playful. "Once again, you get an "F" for failing to follow instructions."

"Come on," he urged. He took a second to point to the picture he helped Star center on the wall. "Look how well I did with the picture."

"Beautiful. You're just the type of man a woman dreams never having around the house," she scolded delightedly.

"You think I'd be that bad to have around?"

"Worse."

"You pack a pretty punch," he answered, chocking to hold down his laughter.

Then without warning, his tone changed. The sense of humor faded and Justin attempted to take the dialogue in a slightly more serious direction.

"I'm glad I came back to see you, Star. I was scared. I thought about seeing you a lot, and nearly wimped out."

"I'm happy you came back too. You wouldn't know but when I was interviewed for the Play Time Magazine article I told the lady about you. I never told her who you were, but I mentioned you had been in my life. She was sure I needed to bring you back...she said it would reveal things to me, clear up things that confuse me."

"Maybe that'll happen. I think if we just let things flow we can see where it takes us...I mean if you let it go, you'll see if she's right."

"What if I don't like where things go?"

"Then you took a chance and it didn't work."

"I don't take many chances, Justin."

"Neither do I."

The room went silent. Star put the copy of the script back on the table.

"Maybe you're correct. What if I didn't get the ending right?"

"You mean to your play? What if we rewrite it together? Come on. You go back where you were with Remy... remember the line?"

Star and Justin both assumed the poses they were in before Justin deviated from what Star had written.

"I'm ready," Star announced.

"If you weren't so afraid you'd actually take a good look." Remy stood, again positioning herself in front of him. In fact, she mimicked the exact pose she'd used moments before, putting her hands on her hips and placing her left foot forward while pushing her weight on the rear right foot. Once more, she was displaying her breasts. "If you looked you wouldn't need to use that fancy imagination of yours."

"You're right. I like what I see just fine," Monte answered enchantingly.

"You do?" Remy shouted excitedly.

"I must have been sleepwalking when you were growing up." He paused to enjoy the enrapturing creature in front of him. "Tonight, I'm breaking every date, dropping every plan. Tonight, it'll be just you and me and so many hours of lost time to make up for. I want to experience everything I've missed all these years."

Monte reached out to hold her by the shoulders, pulling her ever so gently and slowly toward him. Her eyes beheld his face and he stared back; only inches separated them. Gradually that small distance closed and their lips could feel the heat of each other's breath. Suddenly, Star panicked.

"Hold it! Let's take an intermission," she pulsed.

"What's wrong?"

"I'm not sure," she answered frightfully, noticing she was laboring to regulate her breathing.

"You don't want me to kiss you, not yet. I get it," he stated matter-a-fact.

"Look, I simply don't want to let a moment get the best of me."

"I hope I didn't ruin anything."

"Not at all. It's just that my experience dealing with men thus far has been a bit strange."

"I hadn't thought of that. Star, how about we just talk. Does that sound alright?"

"I don't know what's wrong with me. All of a sudden I'm not thinking straight."

"Just forget about the last minute. When I snap my fingers, we'll jump back to feeling how we did before. Ready?"

Justin snapped, seemingly fully aware of the futility of his recommendation.

"I wish...I wished so many times for you to return and now I'm behaving like a foolish child. Look, I don't want to tell you to leave, but I wouldn't mind some time alone. Just let me untangle myself and you'll be the first person I find."

"Then I guess this is, 'see you later'...I hope."

Justin looked bewildered. Star was trembling with fear. Both were having the identical thought. It was a question: *Where Did My Heart Go Wrong*?

It was only a short distance to travel to get to the door. As soon as Justin was outside, his mind started racing. He broke down the encounter with Star into tiny fragments, then he assigned words he thought best fit the experience.

> *I could see as you touched me. Oh, no, your eyes could not have lied? Was I blind? It couldn't have been because I know I could feel your rush. So show me how I lost my touch. Oh, when did I lose my hold...where did my heart go wrong?*

Star at the same moment was surgically dissecting

her engagement with Justin. She also used words to create phrases that she believed best described her inner struggle.

> *I just don't understand myself anymore. It all felt so right. Why couldn't I break my chains, and set my soul a flight? I saw you as you held me; you were like my dream. Why can't I let you in; I just don't see. I know I could feel your rush. Show me why I had to crush it. When did I lose my hold…where did my heart go wrong?*

Justin walked to his car. He was certain she felt as strongly about him as he did about her. It was befuddling because he assumed that Ms. Madam would be the master at handling men. Then as he thought further he realized that it was exactly the opposite. Star was a novice. He was likely the first man to ever show genuine interest in her as a person, as a woman with sensuality and passion. He steadied himself for what he now anticipated was going to be a ride wilder than what she put him through on the bucking bronco—she needed to be broken, but with the softest and gentlest rhythm.

Star was in far worse shape than her lover. She wept tears of regret and consternation. She was emotionally frozen, shocked…traumatized. What was the big deal she wondered? What was so overwhelming that she couldn't cope? It would take several days for her to muster the courage to call him back.

CHAPTER 18: THE TREATMENT

As it is for many humans, the best treatment for anxiety, uncertainty and confusion is to keep busy—Star was a master at following doctor's orders. During the next couple days she worked the girls unmercifully. Like fire drills run by schools for the children to be prepared in case of an emergency, Star would call for spontaneous sessions to review material the girls had mastered many times over.

It was two days since Justin left and she still hadn't tried to reach him. Her mood was foul, the intolerance and scorn she was savagely inflicting on herself she tried to refrain from using to punish the girls. Still, they knew she was troubled and tried their best to be sympathetic of something they had never witnessed from their boss.

It was early afternoon and Star had called for a collective meeting. She had the girls doing mundane tasks such as straightening the furniture and organizing the card table in the main room while she was behind the bar taking inventory.

"Brie, can you help me, please?" she rifled like a bullet.

Star was holding a pencil and pad, scanning the bar.

"Okay, one case of Johnny Black, two bottles of vermouth and three of Amaretto, one peach brandy... and one Rosebank...and..." she hesitated, leaving Brie standing like a statue waiting for the next order. Then Star picked up a bottle of wine, carefully examining it. "Better make it a case of Misty's favorite; she's definitely faithful to Dr. Effington's prescription of wine every night."

While Brie was writing, Star took several glasses off the shelf. Brie must have sensed what was coming, lifting an eye in a motion of disbelief; she was correct.

"Let's go girls. Work today; we have lots to do," she commanded militantly. "We're going to review glasses and drinks again."

As the girls were approaching, Brie whispered to Star.

"No, I don't think you have it down pat," Star responded loud enough that they could all hear. "I don't like mistakes and the other day...I won't mention any names...one of you had an order for a Courvoisier Hennessy and served your customer a brandy instead. So let's snap to it, shall we ladies?"

Star took several more glasses and canisters of spirits

off the shelf. She held up for all of them to see a glass with a long stem.

"We call this a standard—?"

"Wine glass," they answered in unison.

"And this?" Star asked, displaying another similar appearing glass.

The silence irritated her already tenuous mood. "That's why we have to keep going over this. It's a snifter. Remember, smaller taper at the opening. And we use it for what?" Still silence. "Wake up. Brandy. Cognac. Daisy, let me see you serve it."

Star partially filled the glass and placed it on the bar top. Daisy reached but in so doing her hand accidentally touched the top portion.

"Not by the cup," Star shrieked, unnerving all the girls. "I told you, cradle the cup and let the stem rest inside your palm," she instructed while demonstrating the proper use of the hand. "Okay, what's this?" she asked next, lifting a shorter glass with a wide opening.

"Lowball...for sipping," Allie proudly responded.

"Good. Let me see you take an order, Allie."

With a playful smile she approached Brie.

"What can I get for you this evening, Mr. Turner?"

"You mean to drink?"

"Just something to put you in the mood, darling," Allie winked.

"Whatever you think," Brie answered in her most masculine voice.

"I'll bet you're in the mood for a fine scotch," Allie finally suggested after deliberating the choice. "I have just the thing for you."

"I'll bet you do."

"We just received a new McCallan 1975; a palate of sherry and a slow oaky finish as smooth as the silk sheets of my bed."

"Nicely done," Star applauded. "Why don't all of you take a turn practicing taking orders? I'll be right back... girls, I'm sorry. Just a lot on my mind."

After Star left, Allie skipped over to Brie, shoving her chest up close to her face.

"Is there anything else I can do to please you, Mr. Turner?"

"Anything you do would please me," Brie answered, clearly picking up on Allie's queuing her that a sexy, flirtatious skit was in order.

"But what if you ordered a Bloody Mary and I served it in a martini glass?" she lamented theatrically. "Would you think I was a bad girl?"

"I'd be so outraged I'd spank your lovely little behind."

"Mr. Turner, now see what you've done. You're getting me all excited."

Star had been in the office, processing a new referral. Clement Hardy, perhaps the most prestigious litigating attorney in the state, if not the whole of the western states, had vouched for the man. As she sized him up, she estimated he was six foot two and in excellent physical shape, weighing in the two hundred range. She loved to test her skills by guessing what sexual preference the new customers might have.

Her girls all had sophisticated and refined skills in sexual gratification. Each had specialties that Star was aware of and thus her matching a client with one of her people was usually accurate. As Misty had instructed her, Star was rigid in terms of the types of acts she would allow the girls to perform on the clients or have performed on them. Never had one of her people been subjected to any physical abuse. If a man wanted to be tied and beaten she had no problem letting Lena take out a belt and play master. But Star had learned that more often than not the needs of her clients could be handled in a more tender and classic manner.

When she queried the man sitting across from her what he was expecting, she was not surprised that he was vague. Some men were too embarrassed to express their preferences the first time. Thus, in those situations she'd approach the matter in more concrete terms, focusing on tall verses short, large breasted or butted versus small, or hair color, leaving the more esoteric elements of carnal pleasure for a later date when she'd had time to build sufficient rapport with the client for the gentleman to humble himself to her.

She did sense that the man who went by the name of Walt was sad. When she asked if he was married he answered with a tone of resignation, as if a life sentence had been served on him. He also came across as a pressured man who was practiced at keeping his stress beneath a threshold where it might be obvious to others. Still, he was definitely an unsatisfied family man who was suffering from a scarcity of passion.

With the instruction that price was no object, she thought she knew precisely what would lift his spirit. Star pressed a button.

"Hi, can you tell Daisy I'm sending in a man by the name of Walt?" Then she turned to address her new client. "You go through that door. The girls will get you started and I'll be seeing you in a bit."

Walt chuckled, but was silent. The situation seemed bizarre, the most unusual assignment he'd had in his career. Still, he kept his poise, assuming he'd do a careful inspection of the facility, quickly identify the areas of infraction, and then invent an excuse to leave.

He was immediately greeted by Daisy.

"Hi, Walt. Come have a seat."

He did as told, a moment later Brie and Allie rushed over.

"Can I interest you in something to drink?" Brie asked.

"I'm on an expense account...sky's the limit," he jested.

"What will it be then?"

"The best, of course," Walt rejoiced.

"I have just the thing for a man of your taste," Brie swooned at him.

"What's that?"

"It's Red Breast, an Irish whisky so soft and warm that a thimble in your mouth will be almost half as good as a taste of me."

"Sounds like the perfect afternoon treat if you ask me. I think I'll just take whatever the best is this place has to offer."

Several of the girls are now gathered around him, all addressing him excitedly.

"You mean you want...The Treatment?"

"Yeah, right," he smirked apathetically. "Whatever... the treatment is, I'll take it with my drink."

"Did Star approve it?" Allie asked Daisy.

"She suggested it from the start."

"Then you, dear man, you'll soon be ditching that nonchalant shrug." Allie giggled as she turned to Brie and Daisy. "Ready ladies?"

Like a well-drilled team, they went into action. Brie reached for the lever on the side of the chair Walt was sitting on. She pulled it. In an instant Walt's body flew backward, his legs kicking up in the air. Allie was prepared, moving an ottoman for his feet to rest on as they came down. His body was in a prone position but before he knew what was happening Monica, one of the other girls, had his drink and was holding it for him as he sipped.

Daisy by this time was busy massaging his hands and Allie was working the neck. Brie had gone for a pair of slippers. When she returned, she gently removed his shoes and replaced them with the fur-lined comforters. Once his feet were taken care of she brought a blanket. She laid it carefully over his body, tucking it in around him.

"One at a time on the feet," Daisy reminded Brie. "Make sure your hands are warm. We don't want Walt getting chilled."

With Brie assigned the feet, Monica was free to address his face. She had a steamer with several warm cloths inside. She began softly wiping the grease and sweat that had accumulated during the day, refreshing the skin with a orange spice fragranced liquid.

Enjoying the unprecedented attention of four women, each exceeding in charm, beauty and sexual appeal of most ladies he'd ever seen, he felt as if he was bathing in a vat of rejuvenation spirits. All he had to do was tilt his head forward and his lips were moistened with a taste of a liquid that seemed to improve in quality with every swallow; he drank freely, losing track of how much alcohol he was consuming.

In his state of bliss, he felt a vibration in his pocket. At the same time a chiming sound began, the familiar tone a most unpleasant intrusion he favored ignoring. No doubt he would have...except...he was conditioned to never let a call go unanswered.

"Shit, that's mine," Walt grumbled. "Girls, the phone is in my pant pocket."

Brie reached to get it, flipping it open for him.

"Let me hold it for you, Walt," she said with sweet obsequiousness, positioning the cell next to his ear.

"Hello," Walt answered.

The girls tending to Walt, fortunately, could not hear the conversation between Walt and the man paying for his treatment, Hugh Crawford.

"When are you getting over to Misty's?" Hugh questioned.

"Right now."

"You mean today?"

"No, presently," Walt evasively responded.

"Oh, you're there. I see."

Allie looked adoringly at him, rubbing her hands gently through his hair. "I love the way your hair waves," she whispered.

"Exactly," Walt answered, smiling through Allie's lavender fragranced flowing hair that was brushing his face.

"How's it going?"

Allie now lifted her leg over Walt so that she could straddle him like a horse; she was then facing him.

"Is everything okay?" she asked softly into the free ear.

"Fantastic. It couldn't be better," his response serving perfectly to answer both Hugh and Allie.

"Did you find anything yet?" Hugh posed.

"It's a little hard to...what did you say?

Monica had by then taken over his feet and was massaging. She scooted Allie forward so that her partner's crotch was nearly in Walt's face. Then Monica lifted the blanket and unbuckled his belt, pulling it off and tossing it randomly. She unclasped his pants next.

"Walter? Can I call you Walter?" After he nodded affirmatively, she continued. "Walter, I'm just going to slip these off, if you don't mind—wouldn't want to get them wet." In an instant she yanked off his trousers. "We're going to make this the first day of the best part of your life." She was already steaming his feet.

"Did you find anything? Can't you hear me, Walt?" Hugh asked a second time.

"I'm working on it. By the time I'm through I believe I'll know every detail."

"That-a-boy. And don't forget, no budget," Hugh boasted.

"Good. I don't think you can get this taken care of cheap."

"I promise you, son. Nothing is ever cheap at Misty's," Hugh attested.

"I can see why, sir."

"Now let's get together as soon as you're finished; I'm counting on you."

"I'm your man," Walt beamed, signaling to Brie that the call was finished.

Star walked into the room. "The ladies are taking good enough care of you, I hope, Walt."

"They say they're giving me The Treatment."

"That's not quite the truth. Sometimes my girls can be naughty and make up stories."

"Wow. There's more?"

"Quite a bit. Let's say we call this Part I of The Treatment."

"My Lord, I don't want to miss a thing," Walt exulted.

"That's why I'm here; to make sure when we complete Part II you're not feeling cheated. These dolls will give you anything you want today. So tell me now, Walt, since you seem a bit more relaxed than you did when you arrived, do you have any special interests I should know about? You know, we all have secret wishes we'd like satisfied."

"I guess I'm the same as anyone else who comes here."

"But not every man comes for the same reason."

"They don't?"

"Actually, every man comes for a different reason. That's what Part I is about. We want to help you figure out what your deeply hidden dream is."

"I'm trying."

"There's no hurry. But let me give you some hints."

Star's performance was worthy of an Oscar. She was an accomplished actress, a seductress in her own right. Her voice was soothing, intoxicating, hypnotic and erotic. She stimulated sexual drive, but not in the manner of her girls. They relied on enticing and revealing outfits, tantalizing hairstyles and make up applied to signal eagerness, boldness, coarseness, crudeness and indecency. For Star it was that she exuded a mystique. It was a natural endowment, a perfect complement to her role as the warden of sex.

What was most astonishing was that as she acquired more and more of the skills of her trade, she not only became better at practicing it but more comfortable. At a point it came to her awareness that generally she was not on stage playing a role but instead, like a Zen master, she had become one with her mission.

"Walt," she awakened his attention. "Some men come here for pure physical pleasure, some come to bury the agony of loneliness, some want a moment's relief from whatever is torturing them in their daily life, some... some come because they want more exotic types of satisfaction that they have nobody to pleasure them with."

"Like what?" he sighed.

"Walt, all of my girls can do almost anything, but they each have unique skill sets. If you needed a knee replacement, a heart surgeon could do it but the fittings might end up a bit loose. Pay attention now," she suggested, patting Daisy on the shoulder. "Daisy here is a soft soul with a tender touch that'll ease you to serenity." She stepped closer to Brie. "Brie...well, Brie has a tendency to be rough, I won't lie. She can handle delicacy if she has to but her nature is to dominate a man to total submission; she administers humiliation rather than brutality.

"Now Allie, who you know well by now, is an intellectual, a conversationalist, a real companion for a loquacious type." Star chuckled. "Some of the most impotent men on earth have left here healthy sex animals after a single evening with her—a born therapist many wives would be grateful to bring into their bedroom."

"I'm not a complicated guy. Just give me something straight forward."

"Let me take this under advisement; no reason to act rashly. I have lots of other girls to choose from if we need it." Star stood, deep in thought for quite some time before she spoke. "I'm certain. Walt, you'll talk with Daisy."

Daisy then raised the chair Walt remained seated in. She reached to lift him up, Walt now standing in his underwear. His upper clothes were unmolested. Instinctively he reached for his pants but Daisy beat him to it, holding them with her left hand while clasping Walt's left in her right. She led him to a couch and had him sit next to her.

"Someone forgot to loosen you up," she said sweetly, cozying up to him as she reached to pull off his tie and then unbutton his shirt collar. "When it feels s o o o good, what's to worry?"

Daisy next crossed her legs, one over the other, stretching the left so that it rested on Walt's lap, proximate to his groin. She beamed adoringly. Walt anxiously squirmed, trying to reposition his body. Daisy, noticing his discomfort, took both of her hands and touched his face tenderly.

"I can detect the slightest changes in body temperature," she warned him.

"Oh," he squeaked.

"Yap." She held her fingers gently on his cheeks. "That feels like about a one degree increase right there."

"Really?"

"Come to think of it, Walt, a lot of men who come to see me end up running dangerously high temperatures."

"I can see why," he said meekly.

"I'm not making them sick, am I?" she questioned apologetically.

"Not quite."

"Now the next time I feel you, if you're burning up I think I'll have to take you to bed."

"If only my wife..."he responded dreamily.

Daily now took her two long ponytails and crossed them behind Walt's neck, drawing his face to the space between her half revealed breasts.

"She doesn't give you the royal treatment?"

"No, she gives me the royal boot."

"As long as I get a good 'I love you' every once in a while I'll give my man what he needs," Daisy sighed.

"I told her I love her...eighteen years ago when we got married."

"Well, that may be a big chunk of the problem. I

can't speak for all women, but me, I'm really not hard to please. Walt, you know what I say to a man?"

Walt shook his head to indicate he didn't.

"You treat me right *and I'll Wanna Give You the World*. You want me to tell you about it, dear?"

Walt nodded and Daisy proceeded to deliver to him a lesson he'd have never learned if he attended psychotherapy for the duration of his life.

"You see, I have as simple of needs as you could ask for," Daisy began. "Well, if you smile 'til I glow, just once in a while or so, and you watch my eyelids twirl, then I wanna give you the world. And if you brush me on the chin, just once every now and again, so I feel like a little girl, then I wanna give you the world."

Daisy stood up as she continued her dramatically enacted speech.

"Here's the big surprise, Walt. I don't need no jewelry and I don't need no pearl, just show me some of that foolery and I'll wanna give you the world. I only feel my heart beat goin' when you're holdin' a basket filled with a daffodil and the sweet scent of all my thrill."

She now moved back close, cuddling up to him.

"There's more, darlin'. Now if you slip my coat off slow, when I stumble in from the cold, it'll make my tummy twirl and I'll wanna give you the world. If you touch my hand so soft, underneath the tablecloth, 'til I blush like a little girl, then I'll wanna give you the world." Daisy's eyes glistened from the unexpected moisture filming them. "Look what you did to me. You got me teary-eyed, Honey. You got me dreamin' like a little child…it's true. So even if it's just for a little while, I wanna give you the world."

The truth of her words left a gleaming smile wrapping across her face. Walt sat for a moment; then he jumped to his feet.

"You know what?" he proclaimed. "I'm going to give it a whirl."

"You're ready for The Treatment?"

"Oh, I want it; I can't wait for it."

Daisy sensed an odd change in Walt's condition. She reached the back of her hand to touch it to his forehead.

"Walt, you're freezing now. You sure you want it… here…now?" she posed to him peculiarly.

"I'm thrilled at the thought of it. You are the best sex therapist in the world. My wife and I have gone to expert after expert and every time I've left flat, no more interest in her than a wart. But…you did it. I'm sorry, but whom am I kidding? I have to go home."

Walt cinched up his pants, buttoned his shirt and straightened his tie. He hugged Daisy and left.

CHAPTER 19: CLUTCHING DREAMS

It took an unimaginable amount of courage for Star to pick up the phone and place a call to Justin. He'd written his contact information on a piece of paper before he left her the last time they met. When she finally reached him, it was a short conversation, very brief in fact. Star informed him that she was ready to see him again and needed to discuss a problem. She mentioned a time and day. Justin answered that he'd be there; neither wanted to say anything that might stir doubt on her behalf.

Star was in the main hall, finishing a floral arrangement when she heard a tap on the door. She watched as it slowly opened, Justin letting himself in. They eyed one another. Their passion was hungry and their appetites greedy for lust. Both had been short-changed the valor to act on their passion.

"Hi," she greeted him with a warm smile. "Thank you for coming."

"Star, all I want to do is be with you. You mentioned that something was wrong."

"Yes. Something is wrong with me," she admitted, riveting her eyes on his pure skin and marveling at his long blond lashes. "I don't want to let you go, ever. I just can't let you in. Will you be patient with me?"

He reached for her hands and they stood grasping one another. He was about to assure her he'd already waited almost a decade for her and was prepared to do the same again for her love, but he was interrupted by an unexpected intrusion.

Misty ambled into the room, mumbling inaudibly to herself. As she looked up to see the two young lovers holding hands, she stood in horror and was unable to control her reaction.

"What the hell is going on here?" she blurted out angrily.

"Nothing...and what business is it of yours?" Star struck back in an unprecedentedly harsh manner.

"This stops, right here," Misty demanded.

"Misty, what is so terrible about a friend, especially a male one?"

"Justin. Star and I need to talk. I think it would be best if you left."

Justin looked hesitantly at Star, but received no counter instruction. "Star, call me."

The door hadn't even closed before Misty challenged Star.

"A young woman at your age and a man well into his twenties are never just friends. So what then?"

"I like him...I liked him when I was twelve. I want him in my life," Star protested.

"Sure. Go ahead. Ruin everything."

"Ruin what?" Star shouted. "I'm going to ruin your fantasy to keep me here, for yourself, forever?"

"I never stopped you from leaving," Misty bitterly shot back.

"But you never took me anyplace, did you? All those years, never once?"

"Why should I? You were content; you were as happy as any child. I'd say, in fact, you had it a hell of a lot better than most children," she reminded her. "You had nothing but love. Every dream you had I made sure was filled for you. Did it matter if it was here or elsewhere?"

Star's chest was heaving. "How could you know what I was dreaming? Did you ever ask me?" she screeched defiantly. "What if I dream now to wander? What if I dream of love, for me, real love with a real lover?"

"Then wander," Misty sneered. "Throw away everything I've done for you so you can whore yourself around the globe like your mother did."

"My mother didn't whore herself around the globe. No, from what I'm told all she had to do was whore herself around here, for you. Did she die your whore?"

"No, she died the way she lived, like a reckless, foolish, ungrateful and selfish child. She died giving birth to you because she knew she'd never be able to care for you." Misty glared at Star. "I'm sorry. You want to know. She threw away more opportunities than any of my girls could have imagined. Every time she had a chance to make her life right, she did something stupid. I tried every way I knew to keep you from following in her footsteps...and I did a damn good job...at least up until now."

Star was in tears but unwilling to end the conversation.

"I don't get it. I let a man for the first time into my world and there's a whole new you."

"He'll use you and then move on to the next conquest. Why throw away everything you have for some—?"

"Yes, I remember your lessons on men. *Now you listen to me, Star. Men can be great...but don't ever let 'em ever too close to you hun, they're all bums.* All of them, Misty, or just the ones who fouled up your life?"

"I learned my lessons the hard way," Misty retorted with an unexpected calm, given the cruelty of Star's words. "You want to do the same? Then go get all the life experiences you need. But let me tell you one thing and you listen to me," she cautioned vigorously, "not with that one. I'm warning you, and don't test me."

"This is the only one you told me not to hate. You told me he was different from the rest. Don't you remember?"

"Forget what I said: I forbid you. I hope you hear me,"

she said with an eerie softness to her voice. "I forbid it!! Star, I love you. I'm trying to take care of you. You're still a child and I want to protect you from unimaginable hurt. You need to trust me; please, Star, just this once."

Star's watery eyes couldn't focus. She ran out of the room, leaving Misty alone. Misty was wounded. She'd never attacked Star before and never had the girl speak out to her with such disdain. Exhausted and resting back in a chair, Misty was swirling in riddles. She should have seen it coming from the start, never let Hugh's son even visit the ranch let alone tinker with him meeting Star. Now what could she do? Was there an answer? Misty ruminated on the puzzle for hours.

Is there a way I can take her from her hopeless lovin'? How can I tell her that it's impossible, unthinkable, that it's purely inconceivable? Was there some time ago when I could have seen this, when I could have stopped her from the thrill of lovin' him? Surely no.

Misty understood the potential for treachery, yet this time she was certain that what she had observed was not a plot being orchestrated by Hugh. Still, however the drama was being directed, the production had to be ended...forever.

CHAPTER 20: ANATOMY OF A WHORE

The world of elegance and glamour was not foreign to Gyps. Even before she worked for Misty, she had earned the reputation as a top-of-the-line hooker. Her clients included wealthy businessmen, entertainers and politicians. The only reason she settled in with Misty was to try and bring stability to her life.

Not infrequently she'd be invited on trips to distant locations and provided with a lavish budget to dress in the latest fashions. Fine jewelry was given to her and tips were plentiful. But she squandered the money foolishly. If she was unhappy with her apartment, she might pick up and leave after a month, having spent thousands decorating it. Typically she'd abandon not only the props she'd purchased, but the clothing and often the jewelry as well.

When she wanted to move, she took with her the

clothing she was wearing and her cell phone. It gave her a sense of freedom to be able to walk out on one life in the morning and purchase a new one in the afternoon. She was hoping when she hooked up with Misty that a fixed setting would settle her down.

That was never accomplished until oddly when she became pregnant. Before that, she was constantly struggling with fleeing; on several occasions she'd disappear for days at a time, inciting Misty's ire—accepting her back was one of the things that mystified her colleagues in that such behavior would have never been tolerated if it had been anyone else.

Yet once she was with baby, Gyps noticed a feeling of fulfillment and contentment such that she had never known before. Rather than wanting to ditch the growing organism inside her, she saw it as a blessing, something to feel attached to and something that gave her a sense of being grounded. She concealed as long as possible that she was going to have a baby, all the while fantasizing that at last she would have the opportunity to redeem the wrong she had done in her life.

But then as her mornings began to sicken her, her appetite started to be challenged by bouts of nausea, and finally her belly elected to swell and she'd have episodes of sweating and panting—noticing changes in her psyche as well—a change of heart took place. Her confidence waned. She found herself ruminating about what she was going to do with an infant, wondering how she'd do the feeding, diapering and nurturing for the baby.

Then as time progressed, her apprehensions graduated to fear: occasionally she'd experience panic and terror. It was the feeling of entrapment, and then the irrepressible sense of needing to unburden herself of an invisible intruder. She dreamed—daytime fantasies and nighttime nightmares—about escape. The images in her head rehearsed acts of trying to run, only to envision slamming into walls. Repeatedly, she sensed she was locked into cell-like enclosures and was screeching to get out, with a screaming monster barking at her heals. That's when her legs would turn to jelly and she'd fall helplessly on the ground, after which the fiend in pursuit would smother her.

Even while this internal torment was unfolding— during the period of time after Misty had put her out but was still overseeing her care through the final period of the pregnancy—she'd argue with Misty to keep the baby. In response, her boss would chastise her for being such a fool to believe she'd be able to nurture an infant after so pitifully wasting her own life. Disgusted with herself, Gyps would in the end be defenseless to protest against the heartless condemnations of Misty—how could she, knowing that they were true? No wonder, by the time she was due to deliver she had no choice but to take the offer proposed to her.

Gyps would disappear—the caveat being that she was

never to return. She had been banished from the ranch—relieved of any responsibility for her child—in exchange for never trying to make contact with the baby or Misty or anyone associated with the ranch. The verdict had been handed down. Misty had expelled her from her life, once and forever.

Now as she looked in the mirror at her luxury condo, contemplating which of her newly purchased outfits she was going to wear, she rehearsed every word of the verbal contract she consented to with her ex-boss. Her heart had been broken, but would it be forgivable for her to return, likely crushing a child by revealing to Star the true history of her weak and deplorable mother?

She couldn't justify it. Still, she'd hatched an approach to set everything in order.

Gyps had stripped off her clothes and taken a bath. After soaking in the tub for an hour, she showered. There was a giant mirror that hung floor to ceiling in the bathroom and she stood in front of it. She closely inspected her body, shocked to discover that after all the years of wandering, at times lacking food, neglecting exercise and proper sunlight, she seemed as dazzling as she had been during the glory days of her working.

She stood straight, about five-foot six inches. Earlier that day she'd called a salon and had her hair trimmed and blown dry. That was followed by a facial treatment. She'd twisted her freshly cut hair into a bun to keep it dry while she bathed—pulled it back and out of the way she took note of the length and thinness of her neck. Her breasts had retained their fullness and form, the nipples large, honey-colored and firm; weapons she'd always used to disarm the male defenses.

While in the tub she'd shaved every bit of hair from her body other than that on her crown and face. The clean, fresh and smooth look of her groin excited men's imagination and she recalled, in particular, the madness her customer's experienced seeing her in the raw for the first time.

Then as she examined herself more closely, especially her face, she was pleased to see that the cold callousness she'd relied on to exploit men had not been forsaken. She was going back into business, to provide the only service she was capable of delivering. It was a hardhearted enterprise, one she was well suited for. She yearned for the thrill—not for money but for the delight of conquest. She needed to practice, practice, over and over, in preparation to carry out her ultimate mission.

In the bedroom, she had laid out the numerous garments and shoes she'd purchased. She chose a black dress, tightly fitting the upper and lower body but cut short at the thighs. Around the waist she placed a loosely fitted thin red belt that matched the high heel shoes. She dangled from her ears colorful feather earrings and around her neck she clasped a sheer silver chain. Her purse was long and thin. She tucked it under her arm.

She took a cab to Caesar's Palace and sat at The Shadow

Bar, ordering a mango margarita. About a half hour later, a gentleman sat down and began talking with her. He was a handsome man who within five minutes invited her to his room. She stood up and sneered before yelling to the bartender to please have the man stop bothering her, informing him that her husband might not take kindly to her being hustled.

She sat down to finish her drink, laughing at the amateurishness of the hotel employee not to recognize that once she established herself as a married woman she'd be left alone to hustle business unmolested. Gyps had been through the routine years before and not forgotten a trick. Still, after a short time, she noticed that she was bored. She decided to pursue her endeavor elsewhere.

She made her way to the front door and left. Her plan was to mosey down the block to the next hotel; it wouldn't be necessary. A man in his forties approached her from behind.

"Nice maneuver," he chuckled. "Well done."

"I do a lot of things well," she responded seductively, certain that this handsome creature had no interest in harassing her.

"I can tell that by looking," he smiled.

His hair was wavy and dark, his skin creamy and smooth. She noticed around his neck an expensive gold chain and a Rolex watch on his right wrist.

"I'd be delighted if you'd accompany me for dinner this evening," he proposed.

"I don't do dinner. But I'll tell you what. Get us a cab and I'll take you back to my place. I prefer not wasting time."

"What's your name?" he asked.

"You can call me anything you like," Gyps smiled. "I prefer something earthy, like Terra."

"Salt of the earth? I'm mineral deficient."

"You won't be when I'm through with you," she promised.

It was the same routine every night, every afternoon, at least twice a day. She honed her skills, complimenting herself on how quickly every ploy came back to her. Even the muscle movement she'd worked so hard to master was intact. It was a talent few women could attain, one that distinguished her such that once a man had been exposed to her love, they would forever yearn to return; and pay any fee for the privilege.

Once the man's organ entered, she deliberately applied pressure in a rhythmic pattern starting with the outer most area of the vagina and progressively working inward. She was able to tighten like a vice around the man's erection, squeezing with any degree of pressure she felt necessary to elicit the greatest measure of excitation. By the time she choked off the tip with her deeply buried set of internal muscles the subject cried for mercy, screamed his deepest pains and revealed his innermost secret wishes—he was hers to do with as she pleased from then on.

However, this time around there was one difference;

no client was ever getting a second shot. They were to be mere props in a rehearsal. Gyps was preparing for the opening and final performance. Thus, she had a speech she delivered at the end of each session.

"It was nice, Martin. There's no charge. Now get out and I don't want to ever hear from you again. If you come to the building, I'll have you thrown out. Do you understand?"

Some begged. Some offered immense enticement to bargain a change of heart. Some argued. One cried. Only one objected vehemently, insulted by her authoritative tone of voice and scornful attitude. The man went so far as to grab at Gyps, an act she was prepared for.

She kept her purse by her side. Recognizing his anger and potential to turn violent toward her, she picked it up. As he reached for her, she pulled out a knife about five inches long, his forearm intercepted by the razor thin steel blade. The blood was pouring out. The man stood shocked. She threw him the towel he'd used to wipe himself after his climax. She opened the door, and pushed him out.

Every time she went on a new adventure, she wore a different outfit and tossed them in the corner of the closet after she finished. She never used the same one twice. Gyps was a wealthy lady. The interest alone on her money was replenishing any funds that she could spend.

There was one costume in her new wardrobe that she kept aside. She was saving it for a special event.

CHAPTER 21: NOT EVEN CLOSE TO ALMOST

Hugh Crawford was an old-fashioned fellow at heart. In fact, he displayed no shame in referring to himself as a neo-Luddite. The man despised most every modern convenience, all of which he abundantly possessed in the newest and most advanced form—his only observance of a prior period of simplicity was the outdated corded phone on his desk, one with a perpetually tangled cord.

He had his wife on hold. She was listening to him curse that the new twenty-five foot line his secretary had recently purchased for his receiver had defied him by shriveling up to a lousy seven feet. The damn thing looked like a mutated genome.

"Hugh, they do make portable phones," his wife sweetly reminded him for the millionth time.

"They cause cancer, my love. You wouldn't want to lose me so soon, would you?"

Attempting to humor his way through the exasperation of listening to his wife, his mood worsened when his secretary informed him that both Walt and Obbie were on their way to see him. When he noticed the door open and then both of the men enter, he motioned for them to sit.

"Yes, dear," he snarled. "Yes, dear. I heard you, precious." He paused several times as she rattled on. "Yes, for sure, dear. Okay, dear. I really must go, Smoochy. When I get home, love. Now, I have to hang up for a meeting, my love. No, not at all, dear; no I'm not upset," he kindly answered, motioning with the receiver that he wanted to pound it on the desktop. "I promise, pumpkin, the minute I get home." His aggravation evident, he finally hung up.

"Oh, give me a drug, please," he heaved as he stared at the twosome.

"Should we come back?" Obbie asked politely.

"Should *we* come back?" he aped. "You must be conspiring with my wife to drive me crazy, Obbie." He stopped to process a faint recall. "Didn't I ban you from my world, you hopeless termite? Ah, what's the use? Marriage, gentlemen...it never allows a good fellow like me a moment's peace."

"It's better than nothing at all. It is better than being alone," Obbie answered humbly.

"Nothing at all…that has a nice ring to it sometimes, my boy. If more men traded in their women for a good bit of 'nothing at all', we'd be a lot better off as a species… the world may even be a more peaceful place."

"That's quite the statement, sir," Obbie blushed.

"Well, it's the women who bring out the violence in men; read Melville and you'll see what the dames can incite in men. It's a known fact; you can trust me on that point. Single's not such a bad way to be. Walt, am I right?"

"Actually, things are much better between the lady and me."

"Lucky if it lasts a day, pal," Hugh chortled. "Now, let's get this nasty piece of business with Misty's over. Walt, how do we wrap this up? I've planned a little celebration for tonight."

"A celebration? For me?" Obbie looked bewildered.

"Not you! The only celebration for you would be if you quit. Walt, let's party."

"Look, uh…I'll be concise. I don't have the heart to put the police on them for some bogus infractions. Thanks for your generous offer, sir, but I'm sorry. I want to climb the ladder as much as the next guy but I need to hang onto a bit of dignity while I do it."

"I don't have the heart," Hugh grimaced mockingly. "What in god's world is going on here? Obbie comes back a sinner after he gets a piece—"

"I did not—"

253

"Obbie, I'm not a fool. Now, what happened to you, Walt? You walked into a whorehouse, got some marriage counseling, and walked out?"

"Pretty much. That and one hell of a good foot rub."

"Am I going nuts? In all Nevada, Misty's has the most spectacular assembly of women. If god handpicked a flock of the world's finest, there'd be no better. And I know from experience that for those women, virtue starts someplace below the shoulders...hell, we all know it. So don't tell me you ate the plate but left the meal."

"Okay...I almost—"

"Almost! A man is not biologically capable of almost."

"I'm sorry, sir, I really am, but I have to disagree. He is...I mean, I did...almost."

"I can't wait to hear what magical turn of events brought you to your senses," Hugh sarcastically questioned.

"I figured out how to get my wife to do the same thing those girls do, only without charging me half a month's pay."

"If I told my wife to do what those girls do, she'd have me arrested," Hugh persisted with his gloomy humor. "It's hopeless trying to talk reason with either of you. But before I kick you out of my office, I want an update. What's going on with this election? All I keep hearing is how your boss is losing...he loses, I lose; I lose and both of you lose," he shrieked, "your jobs...and any chance of ever getting another one in this state."

"Look, it won't come to that. Obbie and I figured out what to do."

"Oh, did you." Hugh's causticity was unmistakable.

"It's simple. Sunshine Ranch is well known throughout the state. Obbie and I already visited—"

"That's the first believable thing I've heard from either of you."

"No, it's not like that," Walt chuckled uncomfortably. "But they are violating several serious ordinances. We could just as easily file charges and lock them up tight overnight."

"Sunshine Ranch is not Misty's. It's not a tenth of what Misty's is." Hugh threw his hands wildly to show his exasperation. "I'll handle this myself. Just get out, both of you."

Walt and Obbie tiptoed out, closing the door behind them.

"God damn it," Hugh grumbled to himself. "I'm getting that daughter out of there if I have to burn the place down myself."

The man meant it. He had an irrepressible determination when he wanted something, shamelessly throwing tantrums no different than a raging child hurls imaginary stars through the cosmos like broken toys. Hugh's spheres were smaller than planetary matter but he had precise aim and no regret for the damage suffered by victims he had designated as targets.

After the bungling team left his office, Hugh's mind

was scheming the destruction of Misty's. Immediately he was spinning his crafty mind to outline a strategy to defeat her. His son, at the same moment, had a far more benevolent goal in mind; he was in love, not a clue that his passion was directed toward his half- sister.

The stable at Misty's was about a hundred yards from the main building where Star's room was located. Misty could get around anywhere she chose, but owing mostly to pride—her ambulation still unsteady—she rarely ventured far from the office or her suite. That made the location where Justin and Star were clandestinely meeting safe from discovery by the woman who had all but threatened Star that she was to can her amorous feelings toward the young man.

The lights were dimly illuminated. Star was pulling Justin's hand, leading him into the room. They sat on the floor, swooning at one another.

"We have to stop meeting like this," Star giggled.

"You're right," Justin agreed, standing to reach for her hand. "Let's go tell everybody right now."

"I can't yet; I need time," she pled.

"You don't have forever; not anymore. Star, I'm moving to New York. This is the dream job, the most amazing opportunity. I don't want what my family has set for me. I have to prove my worth on my own." He looked down at the only woman that had ever enchanted him. "I want you to leave with me."

"New York...New York?"

"Let's live our lives together."

"Don't you think I should muster up the guts to kiss you first?" she asked childishly.

"It'll come. You'll see. You need to get out of here."

"I don't know. Somehow I think it's all dreaming... that I'll never really get there."

"But you will. If you want it bad enough, if you fantasize about it, if you look inside yourself and see how wonderful it'll be, then you'll make it more than a dream." He paused on a thought. "Okay. Just imagine you can't go on living without making your dream come true...all your dreams...and you're standing on stage, in front of thousands of people, seeing the wonders of the world."

He brushed his hand across her brow before attempting to draw her further into a reverie.

"Close your eyes. It's a vast almost endless crack in the surface of the earth. When you walk to the edge you see colors; reds, oranges and yellows, in an infinite range of hues reflected on the walls of the peaks. Like notes in a symphony—instant-by-instant—they change their appearance. If you climb to the bottom of this enormous gorge there's a river. You can glide peacefully along it on a raft but then in a second you'll be drawn through the waters as the pace of the current picks up, even starts to rage," he said softly to build the suspense. "The journey can take you through damp to freezing to sunlight and then to heat, all in the matter of minutes. This place, Star, it exists...I've been there."

"What is it?"

"Come with me and see for yourself; it's only a few hours away. By plane we can be anywhere we want in no time...Niagara Falls, The Statue of Liberty. Oh, there's so much more," he elated. "Now keep your eyes shut...and then take...*Just One Breath*."

Justin spoke in a mystical style, drawing Star further into the fantasy. "Imagine an endless number of new sensations to soak yourself in. It could all becomes yours, in one little burst. Oh, Star. Let's sail the hopeful shores…I'll whisk you off through these doors. We can start on a jet until we see the Everest befalls Tibet; then we'll train beyond to the Yangtze. Or, we can just battle sin until the Vatican. Yes, you can prance through France where you'll find wine and dine and dance, and then we'll breeze to Belize to soak in the sun as we please."

Justin took Star's hand and pulled her to stand next to him as he continued painting a picture of a world Star only knew from books and film.

"Yes, if at first you'd rather we can stay inside the grand 'ole USA, where we'll see California beaches, satin lakes and plains. Dear, it's only a breath from your door if you'll join me."

"It could all become mine, in a moment of time, just one little breath, a few little steps?" Star whispered in disbelief. "It could all become mine if I'm only inclined, in one little breath, I leave this behind?"

"Yes. You can, can't you? You said it!" he cheered. "Didn't you see it? Didn't you see yourself there?"

"Yes. I saw *US* there," she said excitedly.

"Then you'll make it all come true. You're almost there," he encouraged.

"Almost?" she sighed. "I'm always almost. Is there more than almost because, Justin, I can't afford almost?"

Star heard a sound that startled her. Fearing they might be found out, she silenced him by holding her fingers over her mouth.

"I promise to spend every free second I have thinking about this. You'll have my answer soon. Now go," she entreated.

She watched as he heeded her warning. As he left she stood up, noticing her chest heaving and her lungs gasping. She looked upward, whispering to the heavens above, *Just one breath. It could all become mine in a moment of time; just one little breath, a few little steps, it could all become mine; if I'm only inclined in one little breath, I leave this behind.*

Star stood still. She was aware that she was teetering on a precipice but she was unsure if she could jump into destiny's daunting circus. Yet at the same time, she was under the influence of an equal force to stay the current course, one that was stirring emotions she'd never encountered.

Then she asked herself a question: *Could one decision be of such magnitude that a person was rendered impotent to make it, instead left only to pray that some fortuitous event would happen to supersede human will?*

Justin was pulling her to seek a world she'd yearned to explore since childhood. On the other hand, responsibility and obligation, along with contentment and complacency, yanked at her to persist in the sure and steady life she had at Misty's. Then there was the harsh prohibition by Misty, ordering her to stay away from Justin. That warning titillated an unexplored nerve of defiance, while at the same time the ominous warning brutally tore at her defenses, permitting an onrush of fear for what punishment would be sufficient for betraying the woman.

She realized that she had never faced a real crisis, but had been tossed helplessly into a vortex of unrelenting demands and expectations from outside herself. She also couldn't recall ever being a victim of the titanic forces of emotions, thoughts and dreams all colliding at a moment's time, and then calling for action of heroic proportion. Her wish was for an earthquake, tornado or volcanic eruption to supplant the impossibility of her situation. She was in Nevada, the most unlikely location for those acts of nature to save her.

Fortunately, at least for that moment, there were phones in the sin state. The line in the tack room was ringing and she answered. It was a call to duty, a twosome of young men had arrived, eager to spend big. Star had to get back to the main hall. She smiled, thanking god for the break, even if temporary.

Before she was able to reach the room, the team had begun the celebration, acting like college kids on spring break. They'd been to Misty's before, Justin's two buddies, Cameron and Ryan.

"It all starts now, Ryan," Cameron regaled. "Thus begins the night of no memory and no regret."

"A couple of hours at Misty's getting some *l u v* and then to the concert. Spend a little time with the girlfriends, and then off to the beach we go until the sun peaks its head up and starts a new day."

"Spoken finely, Cameron; couldn't have said it better myself."

Star arrived just as the conversation needed a dose of reality. She inspected both of them carefully, sensing she'd seen them before.

"This one is on me mate; take your pick," Ryan magnanimously offered to his friend.

"Hi, fellows. What can I do for you," Star interrupted.

"Wow!" Cameron exclaimed, his eyes bulging out as he looked at Star. "I remember you, but not like this."

"Yes, oddly you look familiar to me," Star answered.

"Many years ago...we came with Justin," Ryan explained.

"You were the two—"

"Yes, ma'am...I mean, madam," Cameron joked. "We

261

are still The Two. That stunning gentleman is Ryan and I'm Cameron."

"And Justin told us all about you...well, not really all," Ryan flattered her. "But we are here on a different mission than our friend."

"How disappointing. Here I thought you came all this way to meet me," Star teased.

"Indeed we did, but we are off overseas tomorrow, to new jobs with new lands to conquer," Cameron noted in his comically boastful style.

"It's our last hooray...at least until we get settled," Ryan giggled.

"Our latest hooray!" Cameron repeated. "We're going all out. After tonight we must take our precious bodies out of the country, and anyone standing in our way we must leave in ruin."

"Well, Cameron," Star placated, "then we will lay our arms at your feet, and beg your mercy to forgive us thinking of repulsing you."

Ryan made a formal bow. "Madam, it's really non-life-threatening. Ah, it's purely hedonistic self-destruction—that's the motto of the day, and there is only one right way to commence this great festivity."

"We love to save the best for the last," Cameron chuckled.

"Yes, the longer I spend with both of you the better I recall you," Star mocked playfully.

"We tend to make an impression," Cameron smiled.

"Indeed, you do. I stood over at that corner of the room watching. Yes, Ryan had a fancy for redheads, if I have it right. And you, Cameron...it'll come to me. Oh, but why waste time on past history. Surely you've both had conquests with every type of luscious lady."

"You are a wise woman," Ryan assured her. "Our experiences are vast and...our tastes are refined. Correct me if I'm wrong, Cam, but..."he switched to an English accent, "ah, we'll be snapping up the best you have in stock."

"You are not mistaken on that point," Cameron concurred, mimicking his friend's accent.

"Let me think," Star deliberated.

"Ryan," Cameron said, tapping his friend on the shoulder to gain his attention, "while she's setting us up, if you'd please join me."

They saluted each other like soldiers.

"We vow..."they began together.

"What is this?" Star broke into laughter, momentarily forgetting the agitation she had brought with her into the room.

"Sit back and enjoy, dear madam. It's our *Ode to Today*," Ryan boasted.

Standing as if delivering a pledge, Cameron began what was clearly a rehearsed dedication to their mission.

"We vow that on this day, we will do nothing that may be beneficial to our good name."

"Today," Ryan continued, "we're gonna do a whole lot of nothin' great, we oughta be a big mistake today."

Star watched as the silly skit with an underlying message of both love and rebellion came to a halt.

"So, in the end you come to Misty's for love. Is that all it's about, love?" Star reflected. "You both may be right."

"What better than that?" Cameron confirmed.

"I think I have just the thing for each of you love masters, a little treat to send you off on your journey as confident officers. And by the way, I like your lines. I like the meaning. It's just what I've been thinking about, ridin' a few ocean waves, leavin' the whole world up in dismay—breaking the rules."

Cameron and Ryan were simple to please. They hadn't grown up much in the years since she last saw them. Star surmised that they wouldn't last long with either of the girls she sent them off with—*they'll come faster than a bowling ball whizzes down the alley*, she chuckled to herself.

Still, she found some of their lines hitting home. *Doing it all wrong, cruising and boozing, leaving the world without shame, getting the heart poppin', moving on to the sweeter stuff*: the message evoked feelings, and she sprinkled them freely like crystals from a salt shaker, wondering if these men still embracing adolescence had provided her the ammunition to finally leap.

She pondered if she was almost there? Then she further deliberated. Was there a place called "almost" from where it was a sure thing that a friend would give you a gentle shove and off you'd go to meet a new life of adventure and opportunity? Or, was almost really nowhere? Was there a rule that you were nowhere until you were somewhere, and the space between the two an illusion, a chimera deluding those stuck between from understanding that "nowhere" was a dung-hole hope had dug for dreamers never willing to risk while "somewhere" was the purpose of living?

It was going to be a momentous twenty-four hours for Star, for Justin, for Misty, for Hugh, for Hugh's wife, for Hampton, and for Gyps—the curtain was about to be lifted for the final acts.

Whatever might be said of her, Gyps would transcend almost; she would also be the force depriving many others of the choice to live in ignorance and innocence between nowhere and somewhere. There was no almost left for Gyps, she'd played those hands for the last time.

CHAPTER 22: MISSION ACCOMPLISHED

The closet in Gyp's condo was filled with extravagant dresses, tops, shoes and undergarments. When she had first gone on a shopping trip it was not without a well-calculated agenda. She knew precisely how many different outfits she was going to need before she'd be left with only one, the costume that now lay on her bed.

She had finished grooming. She took over an hour plucking and shaving every strand of volunteer hair she spotted on her body, oiling and scenting her skin and then applying lotions and fragrances to her face.

Earlier in the day, she'd had the hairdresser visit, streaking her long locks in several shades of gold, brown and auburn. It was parted in the center, cut in several layers descending first so as to cover half of her face and then fanning out to the edges of the neck. It then draped over the shoulders and finally found repose relaxing on the breasts; it was a flowing shawl, waving like a breeze as the head swiveled and swayed yet never forgetting to return to its duty of creating an unimaginable sense of mystique.

Her makeup was applied heavily but in light shades. The effect was to soften her eyes and brows. Contrarily, the gloss used on the lips exaggerated their appearance. She had also carefully selected her jewelry for the momentous occasion. Concealed behind her hair were diamond teardrops in each ear. She wore no rings but had a bright, wide-banded beaded bracelet with a southwestern design in grey, maroon and turquoise on the right wrist. Most distinctive by far was the necklace, actually a collar; it was gold but at the ends it turned to black, the tail narrowing to meet the head of a viper poised to strike.

She made a detailed inspection of her presentation before addressing the outfit she'd chosen. It was quite simple, both in terms of what went into selecting it as well as the act of putting it on. She knew her mission, understood that no other adornments would evoke the male response she was seeking.

No bra; the blouse was a shear black fabric that fit loose but draped the bosom with exactly the amount of weight needed for the nipples to minutely poke through. She threw it on, followed by black tight-fit designer jeans.

The cuffs of the pants fit inside the black boots that rose to just below the knee, the foot tapered blade-thin.

Some like it hot.

Satisfied that she was ready, she left her unit. She'd already made a call. Every detail was orchestrated in advance. All she had to do was stand looking like a hooker outside the executive parking lot at the new Vegas extravaganza—The Great Spirit Hotel—at four-thirty and wait. The rest would take care of itself.

She arrived at twenty-five after, knowing that her date was always precise about his schedule. At exactly the expected time, a black Aston Martin sport coupe roared up the ramp. The man inside paused to make a California roll at the sign. His eyes veered right. He slammed on the brakes. His body pulsed. His breathing stopped before the car sat motionless.

He stared at the image he was beholding; it had to be a trick. He stared at the face he knew well, shocked that the lady's lips partially parted to deliver what he believed was a telling smile, suggesting to him that whatever he was imagining to be true, was. She lingered in her pose. Her resolve was not to quit beckoning him to respond.

The man couldn't reason how but his instinct told him he was being subjected to a ruse, inflaming him to jump out of the car and race up to the role-playing actress.

"I promise you, young lady, I'll have your ass tossed in jail for this. Who put you up to it?" he shrieked, grabbing at her arms.

"Hugh, it's me, Gyps."

Hearing her voice unmanned him. He stood staring at the woman who had to be a phantom. He raised his shoulders and took in a full breath of air, steadying himself against an inclination to pass out.

"This can't be. Gyps...she's dead."

"No, Gyps is not dead. People don't die until they have no purpose to live for; I have a purpose."

"Misty told me—"

"Misty had to lie; it's not her fault. Everything she's done has been for someone else other than Misty."

"She said you died giving bir—"

"I have a daughter; we have a child together. I know that. I walked away, Hugh, like I did with everything that involved responsibility."

"Where did you go?"

"It doesn't matter where I've been or what I've done for the past two decades. What matters is today. Calm down and look at me. What do you see?"

"You look the same as you did...the last time we were together."

"Exactly the same. I wanted it to be identical, so we could pick up where we left off." She smiled cunningly. "What are you feeling? Can you recall where we ended last time?"

Hugh nodded, a sense of faintness again descending over him.

"You don't need to talk much. I'm going to take you to

my place. Then I'm going to put us right where we were the last time we were together. I'm going to give you all you ever dreamed, and a lot more."

Gyps went to the car and opened the passenger door. She let herself in. At the same time, Hugh sat himself behind the wheel. She instructed him to drive.

She had the room prepared. There was no music. The shutters were closed, dim light from two fixtures narrowly allowed illumination. Gyps pressed her body to his, rubbing her chest against him. She could read his yearning, the pent up sexual drive unfulfilled since she last gave him a complete experience.

"It's been a long time, hasn't it? You've not had a woman who has gratified you since, have you?"

Hugh's silence answered a question they both knew was true. Few women can perform feats of animalistic stimulation without shame or inhibition; most men never encounter one in a lifetime though they all spend the duration of their virile time on earth seeking lust at the outer reaches of fantasy.

She began to undress him, part of the ritual they enjoyed in the past. Once naked she laid him on the bed, quickly securing his hands and feet with felt straps she'd set in place before leaving.

"Look up, Hugh," she said sweetly. "I even had a mirror installed for you. I've been here over a week now; all I've done is practice in anticipation of entertaining you. Are you ready to be entertained? I have a new treat for you, just for you in fact. Don't be afraid; you have nothing to fear but your own arrogance. I think you will get past it today," she said softly as she took off her top.

She'd waited for the moment, planned every detail. But she hadn't accounted for experiencing the arousal of her own senses; hadn't considered it, period. The man she most wanted to bring under her complete domination was helpless in front of her, the first part of the mission accomplished. But her body swelled with excitement, a response she knew she had to repress to heartlessly carry out the remainder of her play.

"I'm going to get you everything you ever wanted. I'm going to order you to finally find the satisfaction in life you've been too weak to take for yourself. You know, Hugh, you were never even close to being almost there. You need me. I'm going to get you where you need to go."

"I don't understand," he spoke tentatively.

Gyps noticed his erection lessening. She jumped on top of the bed, standing over him, slowly pulling off each boot and then removing the jeans under which she intentionally wore nothing. She never took her glaring eyes off him. She was intent on making sure she had re-established the resolve and dispassion she had moments before—at last she recognized again that cold indifference. It comforted her, secured her that nothing would interfere with what she had to do with Hugh, and then afterward.

"I don't want you going soft on me again no matter

271

what happens here, do you understand me?" she demanded, wrapping her hand firmly around his organ.

He stiffened quickly, staring up at her naked body. "Yes."

"You're a goddamn liar. I promise you will, I know it; you'll turn that thing to a string."

"Gyps, I swear—"

"Stop it. I'm here to help you," she announced, squatting down and forcing him inside her. "Do you remember the feeling?"

"God, I do. Nothing compares."

"Yes it does. That's what you need to learn. You're a foolish, ignorant man and I wouldn't lift a finger to help you if it weren't for the fact I owe someone a favor."

"Gyps—"

"Do me and yourself a kind deed; don't say a word unless I ask you to. You're a tough one, Hugh Crawford, I know all your deceits."

Gyps began working her muscles, noticing him panting.

"Don't even think about it. You have a ways to go before your glory comes."

She leaned forward and reached into the drawer. The silver blade had been placed in a position she knew she could get to. She took it in her hand, holding it out for him to observe.

"What the—"

"I told you not to talk...and if you scream nobody will

hear you. Plus, I don't give a shit. You can leave here today in one piece but you'll have to pay."

"What are you talking—?"

Gyps took the blade and with a ghastly swift movement drew it downward such that she was holding it between her legs: it rested against his abdomen. One small thrusting motion would sever his organ. Immediately he went limp, subconsciously trying to exit the now perceived mortal chamber.

"You lied again. It's important to me that I can trust you but you are unreliable. I promise you this, if you lie to me about what I'm going to discuss with you, I'll put a curse on you. I know you don't believe in evil spirits, but I do. If I were to die, then I'd return to the living if that's what is necessary to torment you worse than this every moment of your life. You should know not to underestimate me by now."

"I think I understand."

"That's good. You fucked me one too many times. Really, one too many, just one lousy time and look what happened. Well, you have to pay for it. There are two demands I have," she stated, touching the cold steel to his abdomen to emphasize the point. "If you refuse me these, I'll drive this blade through your precious cock. If you accept my conditions and lie...I already told you what's going to happen.

"Nobody knows what I'm about to tell you." She halted to prepare him for a sacred disclosure. "Misty is my older sister. She tried with all her might to be a mother to me but I was a rotten thing. My life is not worth dwelling on for I lived only to fail myself and anyone else who cared for me, mostly my sister. She did everything in her power to rescue me. In the end she banished me, and she did the right thing.

"How much can a human being take? Is there a limit to the pain one can inflict on another, a breaking point beyond which a person has no choice but to cut off the source of the suffering? Wouldn't they be redeemed if they did it for their own survival? I took Misty to that point…I could never repent sufficiently.

"So now I have a question for you, though I'm sure you can't answer it yet. You're quite like me, you know? Your character is warped, but you have no awareness of how. Therefore, you can't take responsibility for your flaws. The question? Who is the only woman you ever loved?"

This time she waited for an answer. Hugh gazed up at her, the power monger in repose, submissive and impotent.

"Don't be a coward your whole life, for god's sakes. Say it's me and I'll slit your throat instead of your dick," she smirked. "Tell me it's your wife and I'll just laugh in your face. No, you keep guessing."

Gyps stood up, leaving his limp body to deliberate on a question she knew he had the answer to, but had buried deep in his soul. It was fear and insecurity that prevented him from ever outwardly admitting it.

She went into the bathroom to relieve herself.

"See what happens when you spend your entire life lying? You can't find truth even when it's in front of your nose. Well, I'll give you a hint. It's the same person I betrayed, disappointed and disrespected. Now, will you finally say it like a big boy, all by yourself."

Hugh did the unimaginable. He began weeping.

"What could I have ever done? She wouldn't give me a shot. And what can I do now?"

"You never knew how to try. You never knew how to be honest. But now you will. This is the first condition you must satisfy in exchange for your precious masculinity. You'll go home and tell your wife you're divorcing her. Then you'll go to Misty and swear your love to her, tell her you'll repent to her for the rest of your life if necessary to have her." Gyps smiled. "I know what she looks like. Even after her stroke she's a gloriously beautiful woman, and capable of satisfying you. You always loved her and had you been man enough you never would have got yourself into the predicament you're now in."

"What else?" Hugh asked.

"So we're finished with the first point? Good. Then the second is that you tell Star the truth, that you are her father."

"That's it?"

"Tell her the whole story, including that you were with

me only because you were too ungallant, too unworthy, and too uncourageous to pursue the woman you loved all along. Tell her you were using me to hurt Misty, to arouse her jealousy, to punish her for nothing more than being smarter and stronger than you.

"It's our child but she belongs to Misty. My sister has too much pressure on her; that's probably why she had the stroke—everybody has a breaking point. Help her out; Star will survive. She has to be stronger than me; she had love all the way. That's what gives a person the strength to endure, love."

"I'll tell her everything; I swear it, Gyps," Hugh vowed.

"You say you will now, but you're weak-at-heart. In no time, you'll begin playing with the conditions of your contract, looking for loopholes to cheat me. But I promise you no matter what you find out in the next twenty-four hours, if you betray this trust, I'll come after you and you won't get off this easily."

"No, not this time. I did love Misty; I still love her. She's the only woman I ever met that I respect. It's killed me to see her hurt."

Gyps stood to the side of the bed. She was stripping off the jewelry and wiping her face clean with a towel.

"I'm going to untie you, Hugh. Then I want you to leave. I don't want to hear another word from you or I'll go in that drawer and take the automatic pistol I purchased yesterday and put a bullet through that dense skull of yours."

276

Her face was flat, her affect undetectable. It was as if she had left the universe of the living. Mechanically, she untied his wrists and feet. He dressed silently and did as instructed. He did glance at her, sending the most obtuse message, one of dreadful concern he knew better than to try addressing.

After he left, Gyps picked up the phone. She placed two calls. The first was to Rothman, her attorney. She instructed him to come by her place in an hour, stating it was urgent. Then she called a number that hadn't changed for the twenty years since she was employed there.

She asked to talk with the chef, Hampton. When he heard her voice he couldn't speak; he didn't have to.

"Hampton, I know you love me. You and Misty are the only two people in my life that have ever loved me and I betrayed both of you. I'm known as Gyps but my birth name is Gentry. I do love you. Forgive me. I'm too weak and broken to make it in this world. Please do me a favor, look after my daughter, Star."

She hung up. She went to the drawer in her bed stand and took out two papers she had prepared. She laid them on the bed. Then she took the revolver and without a thought put a bullet into the right hemisphere of her brain—there was no almost for Gyps.

CHAPTER 23: STAR AND JUSTIN, MISTY AND HUGH...GYPS

Hugh left Gyps' condominium in a swirling state of mind. His instinct was to do precisely as Gyps had predicted and con his way out of a compromised position. In this case, he could still invent a strategic alliance with a satanic partner to defeat the mandate imposed on him—the very concept of acquiescing to an order, regardless of who issued it, was detestable to him.

But this time, he sensed something different. He couldn't discern for certain at first if his inclination to obey was due to the ominous threat made by Gyps should he not comply, or an eagerness on his own part to purify the filthy and ugly world he'd contributed toward creating.

What he did submit to, in the end, was the undisputed verdict that at last he was going to act. The path he would now be traveling soothed him because he believed it had been ordained by a higher power than even he—with all his wealth and influence—possessed. No longer would cowardliness or treachery interfere with a better sense mentality. Hugh Crawford was not in control and it felt right.

What didn't set well with him was a tweaking sense of something horrifying when he parted from Gyps. She had been a play toy for him from the start, yet he knew behind the sex goddess who always possessed a tone of confidence and assurance was a persona of a different order. She was a sad child who had no way of exposing the inadequacies and terrors that she housed in her soul.

He had driven a block from her condo before he stopped the car. He turned off the engine and sat. All of these thoughts were processing through his mind, plus an awareness that beyond his fixation on Gyps' sexual skills and thrilling body, he liked her and had a sort of bond with the girl. He desperately wanted to go back and to share his concern for her. He wanted to tell her the truth how he felt about her. But doing so seemed forbidden not only by her prohibition against him speaking another word to her, but also due to a nagging thought that it would do no good, that Gyps had retreated too far from the living for him to reach her.

His phone rang. He hadn't realized until then that he'd been thinking about Gyps for over an hour.

"Mr. Crawford, it's Jenny," his secretary informed

him. "Attorney Rothman called. He said it was absolutely urgent that I reach you immediately."

"Give me the number."

Rothman was waiting for his call.

"Hugh, I'm at a young girl's condo. I think you know her. You better get over here, fast."

When Rothman gave the address, Hugh mentioned he was only a block away and he'd be right up. He left his car with the valet at her building, imagining that the attorney must have provided a legal service for Gyps. What that might have been, he couldn't conceive of, given that he knew Rothman and his firm as labor representatives that handled cases for his entities.

He entered the unit and saw Rothman seated on the sofa, white in color and with his head down. He looked up at Hugh.

"Go into the bedroom."

"Do I have to, Abe?"

On the coffee table in front of him were two pieces of paper. He motioned to Hugh that he needed to look. He did, coming out a second later with a sick face.

"How did you know I was here?"

"I didn't. But when I read the papers she left I knew I had to reach you before the police were informed."

"Don't worry, I didn't kill her. I'll take care of the police."

"I didn't think you did. Do you know why I'm here, Hugh?"

"I could guess."

"No, you couldn't."

Rothman went on to explain the history of his association with Gyps. He informed Hugh about the millions she had won, as well as that he had discovered after reading Gyps' letter that Hugh was father to her daughter.

"Leave the suicide note, Abe. The other paper I'll take; no sense the whole world knowing the details of her life. I'm sorry you had to see this. The girl has only a few people that will be left grieving."

"I gathered that by the way she was handling things at my office."

"Tomorrow morning I'll straighten this mess out. Abe, I'm going to need a team of divorce attorneys and a boatload of luck. This girl was all heart—too damn much heart for this world you and I are used to dealing in," Hugh lamented. "Half of this is my fault, but you're not in for a confessional, are you?"

"Yom Kippur, clean out all the sins in one clean swoop," Rothman chuckled half-heartedly. "You're too late for me to do it. Besides, Hugh, I'm not your man. I'm a shitty listener, that's why I practice law."

"When I think about it, she was my priest," Hugh muttered.

"Hard to compute, isn't it? All that money comes her way and then she takes her life," Rothman questioned.

"It was too much for her; she's too fragile to tolerate

upheaval of that magnitude. She was always brittle. I should have helped her."

"I'm sorry. I don't know what else to say."

"Abe, there is nothing else. But if I could impose on you for one favor?"

"If I can, of course."

"Get out of here. Don't say a word about what you've seen here until tomorrow morning. I have some business to take care of first, then I'll see to her body."

Rothman stood up and walked out. Hugh sat for several minutes before getting up and closing the door. His influence could arrange for the suicide to be relegated to a single line in the obituary section of the daily paper. There were only a few other people he knew that would care.

When he left, he called his wife and told her he had to fly to San Francisco for the evening and would be back early the next morning. In truth, he took a room at The World Hotel, a gem in his collection of properties. Lacking an appetite, he stayed in. He didn't sleep.

It was about ten the next morning when he dressed and left the hotel. He drove home. It took about one minute to rip apart a marriage spanning over two decades, less than that for his wife to inform him who her attorney would be.

His next destination was Misty's. He pulled in the lot and parked. It was surprising to him that he felt calm, actually excited.

He waited in the main hall for Star to greet him. When she came out, he couldn't help but notice her radiance and charm—he wondered how she'd look in a few minutes.

He had planned to talk with her alone and then request to see Misty. However, Misty caught wind that he was there and invited herself in. They entered through different doors but at about the same time.

"Maybe it's just as well that both of you are here together," Hugh began. "I have a lot to say today and I'd appreciate you both listening before—"

"Before you put this place out of business," Misty jeered. "I know what you've been up to and why. We need to talk about this between you and I...alone, Hugh," she declared sternly.

"You're right. It's because of me you're getting those warning letters. It's also true that in a few days not one client of yours will be permitted through those doors. The reputation of Misty's will be as inglorious as Charles Manson's."

"Damn it, Hugh," Misty shrieked. "This is between us. I don't want Star brought into it."

"Let me straighten out one thing at a time. I took care of the permits and violations this morning. It's over. Business will go on here as usual, I promise...and I apologize for what I was trying to do."

"You're up to something, Hugh. I know you too well," Misty said dubiously.

"I am up to something, and then a lot more than that. I'm up to taking care of every bit of dirt and grime—"

Hugh would have proceeded with another disclosure, if he hadn't been interrupted. What timing. Unknown to him, his son, Justin, was due to meet with Star. They had been planning an announcement of their own. Justin came into the room, more than astonished to see his father—dad no less amazed to see his son. They stood staring, neither at first knowing what to say.

"What's going on here, dad?"

"Dad? Justin, what are you talking about?" Star posed in a nonplussed hush.

"For Christ sakes, Hugh, look what you've done," Misty cried out.

"It's just as well that you're here too son. I had planned to tell you everything later today, if your mom didn't get to you first." Then he took a few seconds to soak in the odd circumstance of Justin being there. "I suspect it might be reasonable for me to ask you the same question, Justin. What are you doing here?"

"I love Star. We love each other. I want her to come with me to New York. It's as simple as that."

Misty and Hugh turned to one another. He could tell she was feeling trapped, realizing there was no escape from telling both of them how they were blood related. She was perplexed that Hugh smiled comfortably.

"Justin, listen to me, it's not simple, not even close to that."

"Dad, we know what we're doing; I'm not a child," he asserted.

"No, you're not. And I have every bit of confidence in you, and you also Star." Hugh paused to eye both of them. His face crinkled and his neck cocked in a submissive pose, as if asking for leniency. "You are both my children. I love both of you equally. You're half brother and sister to one another."

The room was deadly quiet. The details were on the way.

"Let me explain more, if you don't mind. It's in honor to your mother, Star, that I make these disclosures. I want to preface this by asking especially that you forgive Misty for any wrong you might believe she committed. The woman is a martyr. She gave her life for all of us, especially you and your mother.

"Star, Misty is your aunt."

"How did you know?" Misty whispered.

"I'll get to that. I had an affair with the girl named Gyps. It was wrong because the truth is I loved Misty from the start. The whole time, my intent was to arouse jealousy in you, Misty." He hesitantly glanced in her direction. "Misty, I still love you. I told Meg this morning that I'm filing for divorce. I'll do anything to be with you...anything, Misty. I hope you hear me.

"There's more, Star. You have to know everything. Your mother lived after you were born. She had problems in her life and couldn't cope. Misty sacrificed for her and devoted to her more than any human should be expected. It just didn't work out and after you were born, Misty realized that it was hopeless to have Gyps try and raise you. So she sent Gyps away and kept you here."

Hugh swallowed, experiencing fossilized emotions from a forgotten early era of his life. He couldn't successfully shut off the tears accompanying the next portion of his speech.

"Your mother is dead. Her gift to you was to insist that everything be disclosed. She wanted what we all want for you, to make your life as rich and joyous as it can possibly be. Star, she loved you despite the fact that she was never with you physically. Her spirit—a delicate and sweet one—never separated from you. Most importantly, she knew you had been loved and because of that you would take everything I'm telling you and use it to better your life."

"What happened to her?" Star asked anxiously. "I really need to know."

"Like I said, the things that most people might be able to withstand, she couldn't. She won some money, a large sum, millions...most of it is yours, though I doubt you'll need it. Anyway, it shocked her, I guess..."

Hugh couldn't go on. He was overpowered by his feelings, so distraught that Misty came to his side to cradle his weeping body. When he gained temporary control, he tried to answer.

"She...she took her life."

"Oh, God," Misty cried. "She was my baby. I tried to rescue her but she was hurt. He hurt her so bad. My father was a sick man not long after she was born; he became brutal, torturing all of them. Our brother killed himself because of the abuse. Then our mother did the same. She just couldn't take it and left. She ran and ran and ran." Misty's body was shaking. She and Hugh were cuddled together, grief-stricken.

"She never stopped. I couldn't hold on to her. Star, I didn't want you to go through that...she didn't either. For twenty years she stayed away—oh, my little girl. All these years, all I dreamed of was that she would defy me, come back for me to see her and for her to see you. She would have been so proud." She pulled away to look at Hugh. "Where is she?" she squeaked out her words.

"Please, Misty. You can't do this yet. It's too much for you."

"I want to see her," Misty insisted.

"You will. I promise. Let me get everything in order first."

She fell to the ground, lifting her limp head to glance at him wishfully.

"Misty, I'll be with you forever," Hugh promised.

CHAPTER 24: MISTY'S PLACE, LOVE IT OR LEAVE IT

Star was sitting in bed. Her legs were crossed, one over another; she was still in her pajamas. Scattered around the bed top were small journals with strips of red ribbon sticking out to bookmark pages. She read over and over to herself the same passages. She'd chronicled every detail pertaining to Justin, and a lot more from earlier and recent events in her life.

This real nice boy listened to my speech. I wonder what it would be like to go to a real school and have friends around all the time.

My sisters don't believe me, but I'm going to be an actress one day.

That boy, his name is Justin and he's almost in

college. I hardly know him but he was fun to be with. I'll miss him.

I thought of this King for a Night show today and I told Misty and the girls about it. They thought it was a great idea. They were excited that I was going to write it like a play.

A woman from Play Time Magazine, Deze, came to interview me for an article. She told me love would determine my fate. It was strange. She said, "He'll open your heart and you'll find answers to all the questions that confuse you." I can't wait to see what she writes...she hardly listened to a word I said but I guess Misty's speaks for itself.

Justin came back. I can't believe he remembered me. I think he was disappointed that I never left Misty's.

What's with me? I say I want a boyfriend but when he's right there what do I do, I throw him out? He'll probably never come back now.

Justin. Justin. Justin. He keeps coming to see me. When I finally give him a chance, Misty goes nuts.

Justin wants me to go to New York with him... what to do?

Worst day of my life! Finally I think I'm going to make a decision and everything blows up in my face. I'm back to knowing nothing at all. Now I have a father, a brother and millions of dollars. What good is it when I don't know if I need to stay where I am or leave this place behind? I don't know if I need love or I need to avoid it.

Making matters worse, the mother of one of my girls died. She overdosed. I took care of Hollie, like I take care of everything.

Justin left for New York. I still love him. It's different loving him as my brother but I love the feeling of love; I really like it.

Today...we'll see what it brings.

"Hello," Star answered her phone, forcing a composed response. "Hampton?" she responded with surprise. She waited to hear him out. "I'll shower and get dressed. Can you come up in a half hour?"

Promptly, Hampton knocked on Star's door. She went to open it, noticing immediately the sorrow in the face of a man working for her for months that she had hardly spoken to. She motioned for him to enter.

"Tell me what's wrong and I'll see what I can do for you," Star offered.

"I didn't come here for you to help me."

"I'm sorry if I insulted you. I'm just so used to being the one people call for assistance. I assume things when I shouldn't," Star explained. "Please have a seat and then tell me why you wanted to speak with me."

"I know this is a hard time for you. It takes months, sometimes years, wrestling with this sort of loss. Star, I thought your mother was making headway. I would have never left her to come work here if I believed otherwise."

"You knew my mother?!"

"She lived with me for many years. No, we were not carnal lovers, but we were soul lovers. Being with her were some of the best years of my life. I cared for her like the daughter I had but was never allowed to love. Now she's gone. I came because I know there is nobody else who can tell you about her life after you were born. It would be my honor to share what I know."

"Hampton, I have a question. Hugh Crawford—who I now know as my father—is taking care of my mother's will. She left most everything to me, an enormous sum of money I might add. Hugh did mention to me that several million dollars were left to another party but he didn't specify the name. By chance is that you?"

"Yes. I have no idea where the money came from, if that's what you're asking. I did get a call from Mr. Crawford. I've asked him to arrange for all of it to go to my daughter's children."

"You don't want it?"

"What for? How much can I spend?" he laughed.

"Seems the fortune she had is of little worth to either of the people she felt closest to. The whole thing makes no sense to me."

"Does it make sense to you that by chance I ran into the woman who came here to interview you?"

"Deze?"

291

"Yes. She showed me the picture she had of your mother, the one that was given to you by one of the girls that used to work here. When I saw it, I knew that my dear Rose—the name she told me she went by—had a child. How could it be that this strange woman was in the market precisely when I was, and then for no reason she showed me the picture that answered the true identity of your mother?

"I knew all along she was lying to me about her name, and every element of her past. It didn't matter at all to me. She needed to hide and if anyone on earth sympathized with that desire, it had to be me. But I'll tell you, Star, after I knew the truth I went after her. I searched every free moment I had to find her."

Hampton shook his head dolefully. "She was nowhere. She didn't want to be found. She knew exactly where I was. She was the one who saw the announcement that your chef was retiring and encouraged me to apply. But she never called me until the very end. She wanted to tell me she loved me; that's when I knew it was too late for this lifetime. So tell me about making sense. We're always trying to impose reason on randomness—The Man above bellows at our foolishness."

"You're right, Hampton," Star mused. "As soon as I found out about her, my first instinct was to find some deep significance and an implication for the future. Was she going to be the facilitator of my decision to stay here or leave? But all she cared to say to me was that she had never forgot me and I was in her heart all along."

"I hope you find peace. Your mother left this world in that state. That's what I want to believe and that's what I will believe."

Hampton left; it was the first of many discussions that he would have with the young madam.

Later that morning, Deze would make a surprise visit.

"Oh, mon cher, Star, your story is even more tragique but delicious now. I will do another and another piece about you, my young madam. So extraordinaire, my Star, now with romance, a brother, father and mother. I told you love would answer the questions troubling you, didn't I?"

"Yes, but it doesn't seem to be helping me decide about whether I should stay at Misty's. I feel like I'd almost made a decision, but..."

Deze started laughing, moving close to Star and hugging her. "Almost is good enough. Almost is what makes life a dream; it's why life *is* a dream."

After Deze left, Star went back to work. She had finished dealing with an uncomplicated client, had sent the man off for a journey to heaven with Claudette, her newest girl. Star felt a sense of glee, mastery and contentment after quickly honing in on the man's inner fantasy world.

She went up to her room and wrote, the phrases

representing another installment in a struggle that had lingered far too long. She put a title on the page: *Where Else Should I Be*. With pen in hand, she was humming and writing as she composed.

"It seems there's nothing much quite like this little place. You spend a moment in my world and you're in heaven…if there's heaven here at home, where else should I be?

"Joyful faces smile at me, so who cares what the reason why may be. Thrill and laughter roar the night, so where else could I hand out more delight." She sat still and silent for quite some time before the next line came to here. "I hear a quiet voice whisper in my ear, it says I ain't gonna fly away from here." Looking across the room to see herself in the mirror, she spoke the final thought. "Everyone loves my little world, just like it's heaven, so where else should I be?"

She read it over several times. Then she went downstairs and used the piano to play a while. As she did, the words she'd just written became a lyrical message she sang out. It was a rough piece but Hugh, Misty and the rest of the girls applauded her performance.

She didn't know if the approbation was congratulatory for her recital, for having made a decision in general, for having decided specifically to stay for the moment at Misty's, or simply a show of courtesy?

Hampton had heard her singing, by chance standing just outside the room. Later that evening, they talked.

"I'm so relieved, Hampton, to have gotten it over with. I feel like now I can go on with my life."

"Ah, Star," Hampton laughed. "I remember one day after meditating together, your mother looked at me and spoke. 'I think I've almost figured out what to do.' She never told me what it was she was deliberating, and I would have never known had I not bumped into Deze that day. That's when I realized that it had to have something to do with you.

"The point is that I didn't understand until after I lost her that "almost" was fine, that we all live our lives in almost, a place we might escape only for fragments of a second before were back to...almost. Is there a place beyond almost? Do you really want to find it? Almost, Star. It's all about almost, the place from which we live the magical wonders of life's crazy journey. Anything absolutely less or more than almost is an outpost we wander to—sometimes in glory and at other times in agony—and we're grateful to return home to a place from which we can create new fantasies and dreams, ones we hope will transport us away from almost."

"So I was almost in love...I almost left Misty's—"

"Again," Hampton finished the sentence. "I think so. Another Justin might come along and pluck you out of here and then you'll be...almost somewhere else," Hampton smiled. "I still miss your mother," he sadly added. "I almost feel her with me."

"Strange. I almost felt her with me my whole life. I still do…almost," Star chuckled.

Almost never seems like enough. Still, it is the best place to rest peacefully. Too bad it can't last. Star knew she'd have to revisit her future. Her decision to stay on at Misty's was only a pause on the road from almost to…

THE END

OTHER NOVELS COMPLETED AND UPCOMING BY

Dennis A Nehamen

Mistaken Enemy
Insatiable Hate
Mescalero Blood
Crushing Steel
Musicball
DOGMAi
The Making of A Madman
Juliette
The Greatest American Outlaw
Inside Trance
Crushing Dreams

ABOUT THE AUTHOR

Dennis A Nehamen, Ph.D. is a forensic and clinical psychologist who has authored novels, screenplays and musicals, including the award-winning musical *Wrapped*. He lives in Los Angeles with his wife and has two adult children.